In 1851, gold is discovered in Australia...

In China a different scenario is being enacted. A young man and his sister are escaping the Triad, crossing old and decaying roofs, hiding in alleys... but it is not enough.

With his sister killed in front of his eyes, My Li picks up a fallen ring and flees. Pursued relentlessly, he eventually realises he has a Triad talisman of value.

Planning to depart for the goldfields to elude his would-be assassins, My Li is befriended by an elderly Chinese who decides to accompany and guide the young man.

Soon bound for the Great South Land, they are followed closely by the Red Pole assassins sent to retrieve their ring and kill My Li ...

Although a journey of suffering and prejudice, heartbreak and horror, their Chinese pride remains unbroken ...

THE AUTHOR

Jeremy Gadd is a graduate of the Australian National Institute of Dramatic Art (NIDA) and has worked in professional theatre in Australia and the UK as an actor, administrator, producer and playwright. He now lives and writes in an old Federation style house overlooking Botany Bay, the birthplace of modern Australia. He has travelled extensively internationally and around Australia, including several trips to outback areas such as the Gulf country, the Northern Territory and The Kimberley region. These journeys have provided him with the inspiration and material for much of his writing.

The Author has a long publishing history including articles in periodicals such as *The New York Review of the Performing Arts, Dogwatch, the Journal of the Shiplovers' Society of Australia* and *Blast* magazine; some 200 poems in newspapers, periodicals and literary magazines in Australia, USA, UK, New Zealand, Germany and India in *The Sydney Morning Herald, The Australian, The Courier-Mail, The Newcastle Herald, The West Australian, Poetry Wales, Poetry New Zealand, The Salzburg Review, Nation Review, NSW School Magazine, Billy Blue Magazine* & *The Journal of Australian Literature*; many short stories in magazines such as *Quadrant, The Western Review, The NSW School Magazine* and *Town and Country Farmer, The West Australian* & *The Artist's Chronicle*.
Books include the original edition of *Escaping the Triad* - first published in 1998; *Twenty Six Poems* in 2000, '… a distinctive, confident voice', James Charlton, Poetry Editor; *Country* - a selection of previously published short stories, 2008; a volume of *Selected Poems* and the *The Suicide Season* - a novel about wildlife smuggling set in the tropical north of Australia, are to be published by Australian Scholarly Publishing, Melbourne, and BDA Books, Sydney, respectively in 2013.

Published in the United States of America
by
CUSTOM BOOK PUBLICATIONS
SECOND EDITION

ISBN13 978-1-492 388 388
ISB10 1492388386

First Edition
published in Australia, Holy Angels Publishing in 1998

AUTHOR'S NOTE

This novel is a work of historical fiction – but it contains far more fiction than fact. The main characters and events are entirely fictitious, nonetheless, it is historically correct that the period of nineteenth century Chinese emigration to Australia can be traced to a letter from an indentured labourer, named Ah Mouy, to his brother near Canton. The Wentworths, Braidwoods, MacArthurs (whose misspelt name is deliberate) and the notorious Captain Middleton and his vessel, the Dayspring, are historical entities. Middleton was gaoled by the British Government for the appalling conditions on board his ship.

The period background, as depicted in Australia and China, is a fair portrayal of the era and the reference to the Lambing Flat Riot of 1861 is accurate. *The Sydney Morning Herald* report included at the beginning of Chapter XXII is verbatim. The telegraph between Adelaide and Alice Springs, however, was not connected until 1870. For the purpose of the narrative, the author took the liberty of telescoping these two events in time.

I acknowledge my debt to George Farwell's 'Squatter's Castle' (Lansdowne Press 1973) for details of early rural life in Australia and thank the staff of the Mitchell Library in Sydney for their assistance.

'May you live in interesting times.'

愿你生活在有趣的时代

Ancient Chinese curse.

ESCAPING THE TRIAD

A Novel by Jeremy Gadd

逃避三合会

CHAPTER ONE

During the nineteenth century, the ancient political and social institutions of feudal China, ruled for thousands of years by dynastic emperors, were decaying. Intent on lining their own pockets, the Confucianist public service was riddled with corrupt bureaucrats. The peasants were subjected to oppressive taxation so that others might continue to live in luxury they could hardly imagine. China was disintegrating; degenerating into a land divided into districts ruled by regional strong men or war-lords; who, so long as the Emperor of the day received due tribute, were permitted to pillage as they pleased. Eventually, the emperors became so isolated and aloof from the realities of their realm that they found themselves lacking both the military and moral strength needed to enforce their decrees. As the emperors' authority waned, the deteriorating conditions and turmoil encouraged the strong to dominate the weak, and led to an increase in power and influence of the 'Triads'. The Triads – or secret societies – had been part of the Chinese way of life since time immemorial. Their membership was open to everyone and included all crafts, professions and classes. Known by names such as 'The Interlocking Ring', 'The Wedge' and 'The Society of One Hundred Thousand Sorrows', the Triads existed solely for the benefit of their members.

Being a time when the rule of law was arbitrary and cries for justice fell on deaf official ears, injured parties sought protection and settlement of their disputes by means outside of the debased legal processes. The Triads offered instant redress and support for their members. But they also demanded total allegiance, and the tools of their trade included blackmail, extortion, bribery and murder.

In a courtyard far from the walls of the Forbidden City, the palace where successive emperors indulged their whims and from which they rarely ventured, a sombre ceremony once took place. Seven new 'Red Pole' recruits were being initiated into a local lodge of the Triad, and over a hundred brethren had gathered to accept their novice members.

The Red Poles were the Triad's enforcers – highly skilled fighting men trained to kill without remorse or mercy on command of their superiors within the Society. A Red Pole who distinguished himself could aspire to the upper echelons of the Triad's hierarchy.

Their probation period and training completed, the first of the new recruits was led blindfolded into the courtyard, to where the Master of Ceremonies was seated on a dais. The new recruits were each escorted by an experienced Red Pole.

When within a few paces of the Master of Ceremonies, the escorts organised the new recruits into a line facing him. On a word of command from the Master of Ceremonies the new recruits knelt and their escorts moved to one side and stood like sentries behind them.

The Master of Ceremonies gave another order and the new recruits prostrated themselves and then resumed the kneeling positions. The escort behind the new recruit farthest to the Master of Ceremonies' right, stepped forward and removed the black silk blindfold from the new recruit's eyes. The scarf had a Chinese character on one corner.

The escort remained silent, the scarf stretched between his hands as if ready to be used to strangle or garrotte the New Recruit. The other escorts followed his example.

The new recruit closed his eyes and slowly opened them again to accustom his pupils to the bright light of day. As previously instructed, the new recruit fixed his eyes on a spot somewhere over and beyond the Master of Ceremonies' bald head. Fanning himself absently, the Master of Ceremonies appraised the new recruit. He was pleased with what he saw.

The young man appeared to be the right kind of raw material for his role. He seemed self-possessed, strong and intelligent – though, hopefully, not too intelligent, thought the Master of Ceremonies. Men who were above average intelligence or who had vivid imaginations did not usually succeed as Red Poles. Assassins with what would normally be considered to be positive personality traits often did sleep well at night.

Apart from his superficial appraisal, the Master of Ceremonies knew nothing else about the new recruit. The vetting of recruits' suitability was a responsibility delegated to a minion. The Master of Ceremonies was not interested in the reasons why recruits knocked on the Triad's door.

Thus, although he noted that the new recruit was a man who appeared to be about thirty years of age, the Master of Ceremonies might have been surprised to learn the new Red Pole was actually only twenty-five.

The new recruit had been born to impoverished peasant parents and the back-breaking drudgery of working tediously long hours exposed to the sun, wind and rain from an early age had taken its toll. Because of the physical demands of his farming background, he was exceptionally fit, muscular and capable of enduring hardship without complaint.

Years spent up to his knees in the water and slush of the paddy-fields and of gripping a plough being dragged by a wide-horned buffalo had taught patience and made him mentally tough. No-one was better prepared than the new recruit to endure discomfort in the course of his duties.

He was typical of many who sought sanctuary, a sense of belonging, strength through association and at least one square meal a day by asking for admittance to the ranks of the Triad. His family's small-holding had been taken from them by their provincial war-lord, who seized their farm – and their neighbours' – and gave them to his brother-in-law as a wedding gift. One day it was their home; the next day armed men came and evicted them. There was no higher authority the new recruit's family could appeal to; nothing they could do. To object would have meant instant execution. The new recruit only needed one lesson to learn the maxim of survival in his time.

Whoever had the might had the right.

Not long afterwards his mother died. His father said it was because of her broken heart, and the new recruit and his father were reduced to beggary. His father did not long outlive his mother. Petty thieving to avoid starvation introduced the new recruit to the underworld of pimps and rogues, the politically dissatisfied and, the Triads.

Lost in his own thoughts and already looking forward to the finish of the ceremony and getting out of the midday heat, the Master of Ceremonies absent-mindedly continued his assessment of the new recruit. The young man's unruffled demeanour concealed the nervousness the Master of Ceremonies knew he must be feeling. His deep measured breathing as he fought to control his excited heart was the sole indication of the trepidation he undoubtedly felt – for, once a member, the new recruit would never be able to resile from the step he was about to take. Only the dead were permitted to resign from the Triad.

In search of diversion, the bored Master of Ceremonies' restless gaze flitted around the courtyard and back to the new recruit. There was something odd about the experienced Red Pole acting as the new recruit's ceremonial escort; something that gave the man's features an ominous, haughty expression, as if he were constantly exposed to an offensive smell. But whatever it was, the Master of Ceremonies could not tell. The man's cropped head was turned slightly askew from him.

At that point the 'White Fan' or officer in charge of the ritual – and the lodge – separated herself from the waiting members. Resplendent in a white robe with high shoulder-pads and a stiff ribbed collar that rose behind her head in the form of a fan, from which she took her title, she crossed to where the new recruit waited on his knees.

The Master of Ceremonies sniffed disdainfully as the White Fan took up her position. He found it distasteful that he had to obey a woman, even a woman who was as effective, clever and ruthless as the White Fan. The White Fan had worked her way up through the ranks from a lowly decurion and had won the right to provide the executive direction for the Society by force of personality and general acknowledgement that her council was wiser than that of the males around her. But that did not deter the Master of Ceremonies from resenting her achievements.

'Harpie,' breathed the Master of Ceremonies, with more than a hint of jealousy.

'Give me your right hand,' demanded the White Fan.

The new recruit obliged and the White Fan pricked the forefinger of the offered hand. Catching the drops of blood, which glistened in the noonday sunlight, in a small silver bowl, she made incisions in each of the recruits' forefingers before passing the container with their blood to a henchman, who poured rice wine into the bowl and then gently stirred the concoction.

'Why is your coat so old?' demanded the Master of Ceremonies although the new recruit wore no coat and was perspiring heavily.

'It was handed down to me by Five Ancestors,' replied the Recruit.

Pleased with the response, the Master of Ceremonies nodded to the White Fan before returning his attention to the Red Pole escorting the recruit. What was it, he pondered? Without doubt, something about him created an impression of being in the presence of someone capable of extreme cruelty. But the Master of Ceremonies could not put his finger on the reason why. It was not that the man was big and thickset, which he was, or that he wore his hair cropped short instead of in the normal queue or pigtail. Whatever it was, there was an aura of menace about him.

The White Fan was speaking loudly to the new recruit, so that everyone present could hear.

'Do you understand the rituals of the Society and the responsibilities of the position you aspire to?'

'I do,' replied the recruit, 'but I will be guided by my mature brothers and sisters.'

'If officials learn who you are, you will be killed. If you violate the rules of the Society and your position, you will be killed.'

'I understand,' responded the new recruit in a voice that could be heard by all present, 'If I am found unworthy, I shall receive the punishment of three swords and five axes.'

'You will become like this cock,' threatened the White Fan, accepting a white feathered cockerel with its legs trussed from another henchman who stepped forth at the appropriate moment. And she beheaded the cock with a swipe from the short sword she tugged from the folds of her robe.

Another Triad member held up a large stick of burning incense. The blade glittered again in the sunlight.

'You will become like this thick stick of incense,' announced the White Fan, and sliced the incense stick in two.

'Whatever name you were known by in the past is now dead. When you join the Triad you are new-born. We shall give you a new name. You shall be called Yung.'

The new recruit nodded his head quickly in assent and the henchman with the bowl containing the mixed blood and rice wine carefully carried it to where the White Fan stood waiting. After exchanging her bloodied sword for the bowl, the White fan sipped the contents and passed the bowl to the new recruit who copied her. The bowl was then taken from him and sipped and passed on by the other new recruits and their witnessing brethren until empty.

The Master of Ceremonies flicked his fan. 'Before departing, the Five Ancestors composed a verse, which no brethren ever disclose, but if to a brother it is shown, he knows, at once, he is not alone.'

The White Fan bent and whispered the answering secret verse in the new recruit's ear. She then took the black scarf from the escort standing behind the new recruit and placed it in his hands. 'This is yours. It is your proof of membership of this lodge of the Black Scarf Triad. Guard your scarf with your life.'

'Now acknowledge the seal of the Triad,' ordered the Master of Ceremonies. 'Whenever you set eyes on the symbol of this seal, you will know the message to which it is attached is authentic, and must, upon pain of death, be obeyed.'

The Master of Ceremonies dangled his right hand where the new recruit could gaze upon the bulbous signet ring adorning his finger. It was an ostentatious piece that would not have appeared out of place on a shelf in a junk jewellery store. It was fitted loosely on the Master of Ceremonies short chubby digit.

The formal Scarf Presentation and Acknowledgement of the Seal was repeated individually with each of the new recruits. All seven then swore, in unison, an oath stating they were indissolubly joined with the Brotherhood by the bond of blood they now shared.

'You will now await the allotting of your first task,' said the bored Master of Ceremonies, glad the initiation was over and pleased to be able to attend to more pressing matters, most of which were personal.

'Your success will prove your worthiness.'

The new recruit knew the Master of Ceremonies' final words were the end to the ritual and his cue to stand. He kowtowed and then leapt lithely to his feet. The new recruit was ready and determined to prove his worth, for the Triad was now his family. His brethren welcomed him with applause.

It was at that moment the Master of Ceremonies realised what it was about the escorting Red Pole's face that had caught his interest. The ceremony concluded, the new recruit's escort turned towards the Master of Ceremonies. Where flesh and gristle separating the Red Pole's nostrils should have been was a livid, red, unevenly healed scar that twisted his smile into a sneer.

'Whoever did it must have used a wood saw, not a knife,' mused the Master of Ceremonies. 'How amateur...'

CHAPTER TWO

L ater that day, in the same village near Canton, a poor water-carrier received a letter from his brother, Ah Mouy. The Water-carrier had not seen his brother for nearly ten years. Ah Mouy had been the black sheep of their large family. As a restless, energetic young man, he had bravely taken his first step into an unknown future by accepting a contract to indenture himself – selling his labour for a fixed period – for five years to a furniture manufacturer in Mei-erh-pen, or Melbourne, in the great empty land to the south, now called Australia.

At the time Ah Mouy took his destiny into his own hands, emigration from the then Celestial Empire was forbidden. But the seaboard provinces of China were suffering from worse than usual over-population, famine and bloodshed. It was no coincidence the First Opium War and the Taipei Rebellion took place at the same time as an upsurge in the number of Chinese prepared to risk everything, including their lives, in their search for a better way of life elsewhere in the world.

Ah Mouy had to pay his own passage to the Great South Land. The fare was six pounds. Most of his fellow passengers were tradesmen and artisans, not unskilled coolies. Many of them had not been able to afford the fare and borrowed the sum from their village bankers.

They drew up contracts based on family ties and the use of the debtor's wives and children as cheap labour. In more extreme cases, their bodies became security for the payment of the loans. If, after arrival in Australia, the Chinese emigrants wanted to send their earnings back to their families or their bankers, the network of Triads would undertake the transaction in return for a fee. Sometimes the role of the Triads had a more sinister aspect.

The letter Ah Mouy sent to his brother conveyed news that created a furore of excitement and envy as it became known throughout the village. The letter was the latest of several the Water-carrier had received from Ah Mouy. Earlier news had related how Ah Mouy, after a relatively comfortable voyage, by later standards, had served out his indenture with a fair minded European employer. Ah Mouy then become a successful carpenter and made a profitable living for himself building houses. Ah Mouy's brother had been pleased that his sibling had found a new life, but, although Ah Mouy had suggested he join him to share his prosperity, he had never felt the urge to leave his homeland – that is, until he took the latest letter to the village scribe to have it read to him.

The scribe scanned the contents and informed him that his brother had become rich beyond his wildest, avaricious dreams. On the fifteenth of May, 1851, the *Sydney Morning Herald* reported that gold had been discovered near Bathurst in New South Wales. In Sydney and Melbourne, clerks, blacksmiths, solicitors and labourers put aside their pens and tools and walked or rode to the goldfields.

The prices of commodities essential to survive at the diggings soared. The press followed up the initial story with even more extravagant reports of the riches to be found.

'Not only were fortunes waiting to be discovered beneath the earth,' gushed the tabloid columns, 'nuggets lay scattered on the surface of the ground'.

'Wealth was waiting,' so the papers claimed, 'for whoever was prepared to bend their knees'. Left without men to man their sails, ship's masters accompanied their crews to the goldfields. Domestic servants abandoned and told bourgeois ladies to make their own tea and beds and joined the rush. Ah Mouy was amongst them and, luckily, he struck a rich lode of gold. He immediately wrote to his favourite brother, urging him to emigrate.

Ay Mouy's brother paraded the news of his family's good fortune through the streets of the village.

'I'm going to join my brother and become as rich as the Emperor himself! Who will come with me?' he cried in the market-place.

'Where to?'

'To Hsin Chin Shan – the new gold mountain!'

'And where under Heaven is that?'

'Across the Nan Yang – the Southern Sea.'

Many of those who listened to Ah Mouy's brother exhorting others to accompany him across the south sea, especially the younger men, decided that an adventure with riches at the end of the rainbow was more enticing than the boredom of the paddy-fields or shop. They heard the story and, inspired, made their financial arrangements.

The word spread like a grass fire.

Among the throng who heard Ah Mouy's brother was an attractive middle-aged woman. She listened attentively from the edge of the crowd and then left, her wooden sandals clattering against the cobble-stones.

The woman was known as the widow Song Li. Her dress was not the garb usually worn by the peasants. It was a richly embroidered garment that had seen better days. A closer examination would have revealed that the fabric was worn and that rips had been meticulously mended.

In her youth, the widow Song Li had been a courtesan to a great mandarin whose name still commanded respect.

11

But with the mandarin's death, she had long ago fallen from favour, and, destitute, she had married a kindly, elderly soya bean seller, to whom she bore two children.

Her husband had been a good provider and protector but, because his values belonged to an earlier more law abiding time, he refused to pay protection money to the Triad, and – he consequently met with an unfortunate accident – and died from his injuries. Now the widow Song Li knew she too was dying. She had been on her way home from visiting her physician when her attention was attracted to the commotion surrounding Ah Mouy's brother and his letter.

The doctor had confirmed her gravest fears about the lump that was growing in her left breast. By tradition, the doctor only asked for payment when his patients were well. The doctor had begged her pardon at his failure and informed her that he would include her on his list of home visits from then on, and that all future treatment would be free of charge. In a gentle and apologetic manner, the doctor explained that his prognosis was grim. He had seen the condition many times before. All he could promise was a death with minimal pain when the awful time came.

The anxiety that showed on the widow Song Li's still beautiful face as she hurried home was not for herself but for her children. When she reached the corner that led to the house where she rented the top floor with her children, her feet refused to carry her any further. The widow Song Li bit her bottom lip, then turned and retraced her steps. Her route took her across town to the doorway of the house of her landlord, the merchant Han Ying.

On her landlord's doorstep, the widow Song Li paused to catch her breath and compose herself. She closed her eyes and, almost by sheer force of will-power, managed to conjure an aura of elegant desirability about her, which she wore like a visible cloak when she entered the house.

The merchant, Han Ying, was a grossly obese man in his fifties. When he saw the widow Song Li enter his domain, his piggish eyes narrowed. Han Ying had long lusted after Song Li and, nearly every time she came to pay her rent, had repeatedly asked her to become his concubine. To have even the aging ex-concubine of the demised mandarin in his household would increase the wealthy merchant's prestige. But Song Li had always refused him. She thought the merchant repulsive and had lately sent her eldest son, My Li, with the money for the monthly rent. Han Ying had not set eyes on the widow for some time. She had not become less attractive in her absence.

'This is a welcome surprise,' Han Ying said to her. 'What brings you here? It isn't rent time?'

'I have come to take up your offer.'

The merchant's broad face broke into a beaming smile and he reached for his fan to conceal his triumph and self-satisfaction. 'I knew you would one day. I knew it was only a matter of time until common sense prevailed. I was sure the money I mentioned when we last spoke would provide an incentive. Money always helps to make up the mind when deciding affairs of the heart. What is our betrothal going to cost me?'

'The equivalent of fifteen English pounds, and for you to keep me in comfort for the rest of my life.'

'Cheap compared to what I previously offered you,' said Han Ying suspiciously.

'I'm older,' replied Song Li.

'So you are …' smiled the merchant. '… and wiser.'

The merchant pursed his thick lips. 'You have two children and I already have more than enough for one man….'

Hoping to reduce Song Li's already cheap price, Han Ying pretended he had lost interest in the transaction.

'My children are old enough to go their own way in the world. By agreeing to your offer, I am looking after my own well-being …'

Han Ying's pretence and feigned disinterest disappeared. 'It is a deal then,' declared Han Ying. 'When will you move into my house?'

'This day in fourteen weeks' time. It is an auspicious date.'

'Agreed!' said Han Ying, 'send your son over for the money. I'll have it ready tomorrow.'

The widow Song Li returned to her home to explain why and what she had done for her children.

She did not know that the merchant Han Ying was also the Master of Ceremonies for the local lodge of the Triad.

CHAPTER THREE

'You are to travel to the Great South Land and make new lives for yourselves. The merchant's money will pay for your fares and food while you are aboard the white men's sailing ships,' Song Li told her two children.

'I won't go!' her fourteen year old daughter Tiao cried defiantly. 'I won't go and leave you with that… that… '

'That's enough! I am not long of this world. I will soon see the gates of Willow City. But my purgatory will be a short one and joyful in the knowledge your lives will be better than mine.'

Song Li's son, My Li, did not comment. He was a shy and unassuming young man. A youth two years older than his sister, he was an apprentice apothecary and thus aware there could be only one outcome to his mother's ailment.

'What about you My Li, my son? Do you have any objections to my wishes?'

My Li shook his head. His mother had brought him up to respect traditional values and, in a land where ancestor worship was widely practiced, he was not prepared to contradict his mother's wishes.

'No, mother. I do not.'

'Then prepare for your journey as I must mine. And if it makes you feel better Tiao, perhaps you should know that the funds your father left us are no more.

I carefully eked out the amount over the years and budgeted to ensure your childhood needs and your educations would be taken care of – but the money is now finished. My Li will have to look after you now. Unless we do as I have decided, the ditch by the road will become our home.'

'Even a ditch would be warm if we were together,' sobbed Tiao.

Her daughter was a pubescently plump girl who had inherited her mother's pretty face. Her eyes were enlarged from her crying and saddened by the enormity of the events unfolding before her. Her cheeks were wet with her tears. 'Who will see to your funeral? Who will organise the Feast for the Dead and ensure you have rice and gold coins for your journey?'

'I will trust that even Han Ying will show appropriate respect for the dead,' Song Li said to her daughter, and took her gently in her arms to comfort her.

'I will accept whatever is my karma. The deed is already done.' She laughed. 'Besides, I've been trying to out-haggle the hideous Han Ying for years. He's always overcharged us for the rent on this hovel… and if the physician is as good at his profession as I think he is, then Han Ying has a surprise in store for him. Who knows, he has many other women, he might die of a heart attack before he lays a finger on me!'

It was decided that Tiao and My Li would depart for Canton, where they would find a ship for the Great South Land on the day after their mother was due to become part of Han Ying's household. 'My Li will have finished his apprenticeship by then. You will remember to write regularly?' their mother plaintively reminded them, even though it was unlikely she would be alive to receive their letters.

The next day My Li went to the merchant Han Ying's house and collected the money owing to his mother. He heard female voices giggling from inside the house and was aware of eyes following his movements from behind the wooden window shutters. When he arrived home, his mother seemed to have suddenly aged, as if the strain and strenuous activity of the day before had drained her of her energy.

'Here,' she said, her voice tired and hoarse. 'This was your father's money-belt. It has several separate pockets. You must keep the money for the passage inside it. There are brigands and thieves who would slit your throat for a fraction of the amount you will be carrying. Wear it constantly from now on. Get used to wearing it night and day.'

To My Li, the next three months seemed to pass faster than any other months of his life, either before or after. The apothecary to whom My Li was apprenticed was saddened to be losing his pupil so soon.

'I've taught you all I know. You will be welcomed wherever you go as someone who is able to ease suffering.'

My Li thought of his mother, whose suffering was now beyond all help. Unable to watch her pinched grey face and her increasingly vacant eyes as she coped with the pain that racked her now frail body, or to ignore his mother's pleas, My Li was adding extra grains to the dosages of the pain-killers prescribed by Song Li's physician.

The day came when Song Li was due to go the merchant Han Ying's house. She was too weak to walk the distance and My Li had to hire a man and his cart to carry her. Song Li had spent the entire morning employing her courtesan's cosmetic skills to add colour and vibrancy to her ravaged features. Her face, when finished, was like a ghastly mask.

'Our lease here does not expire for another two days, so you have every right to spend the night here before setting off in the morning. Now let us embrace one final time and then go our different paths.'

With her head held high and wearing the patched embroidered dress with the high collar that was her best, Song Li rode through the village to Han Ying's house as the late afternoon light lengthened the shadows.

'Be strong, my children!' she called as they carried her away. 'Be strong, my little ones!'

Little Tiao sobbed unceasingly well into the evening. Before going to bed, My Li made sure that Tiao had packed the one small bag she was going to take with her. After making sure he had included the few changes of clothes he intended to take with him in his apothecary's satchel, he blew out the lamp and stared into the darkness.

My Li woke sensing something terribly amiss. Much later in life, whenever he recounted the story, he swore the reason he woke up was because someone was urgently shaking him, but when he opened his eyes, there was no-one there. He tiptoed into the alcove where Tiao was sound asleep and all was tranquil. For a full minute he stood not knowing what was wrong or what to do. Then he was overwhelmed by the feeling Song Li was present with him in this room.

He could smell the fragrance of her favourite perfume. The one she kept in the delicate blue bottle which she hoarded and sparingly applied so as to lengthen the duration of its use. But Song Li was not present.

My Li heard a distant uproar. It was from the far side of the village – where Han Ying's house was situated.

'Get up Tiao – quickly!'

'What...?'

'Get dressed. Something dreadful has happened! Mother was trying to warn us!'

'Mother…'

'Hurry sleepyhead! We've got to get away from here!'

Tiao and My Li hurriedly dressed. As they put on their clothes, the clamour from across the village increased in volume. It sounded like someone's party had got out of hand and, spreading into the streets, was coming their way. Glancing out the window, My Li could see people carrying lanterns and flaming torches turning into their lane. Now the disturbance was closer he could distinguish individual shouts. Whoever they were they were angry, and then he saw a sedan-chair turn the corner — a sedan-chair attended by armed servants carrying flares that lit the night.

Even from afar My Li could distinguish the bulk of Han Ying the merchant in the swaying chair.

'Find the bastards,' the Merchant was screaming at his staff.

'The whore tried to trick me! She tried to cheat me! The bitch must have known she was dying when she did the deal. Find the young ones! They'll more than compensate for their dead mother. They can take her place!'

Drunk, Han Ying shrieked abuse at his servants. 'Break down the door, you scum!'

My Li snatched Tiao's hand and looked around for an escape route. The alcove where Tiao slept had a small window that opened onto the tiled roof of the communal kitchen downstairs. My Li pushed Tiao through, tossed her bag after her and, grabbing his apothecary's satchel, struggled through the aperture behind her.

The front door to the building below splintered as Han Ying's men burst inside.

As My Li led Tiao across the dangerously loose tiles, he could hear heavy footsteps pounding the stairs within. From their vantage place on the roof, My Li looked down into the lane that ran behind the house in which he and Tiao had lived most of their lives.

Even narrower alleys provided walkways between their house and the buildings on either side.

My Li saw that if they could drop down to the rear lane and clear one of the gaps between the neighbouring houses before Han Ying's hirelings realised what they were up to, there was every possibility he and his sister might reach the maze of dwellings, backyards, courtyards and animal pens, where they might hide or lose their pursuers.

The villagers, woken from their sleep, were staring from their windows and creeping into the street to find out what was happening.

'This way Tiao! Follow me!'

My Li made for the edge of the roof where it hung over the lane at the rear of the house. The paving was only two metres below and he dropped the distance with ease. Tiao lay on the tiles and lowered herself over the edge. Now neighbours were calling. 'What the devil is going on?'

'Who are you people?'

'How dare you make such a racket at this hour of the night?'

'Go back to bed! Mind your own business if you know what is good for you,' retorted Han Ying's men.

'They're not here!' cried a guttural voice from the apartment Tiao and My Li had recently vacated.

As Tiao allowed herself to fall into My Li's waiting grasp, a head appeared through the alcove window. The head had cropped hair.

'I see them! Around the back. Block the lane!'

My Li and Tiao bolted one way up the lane but the sound of feet already rushing towards them down the alley made them hesitate, stop, and then reverse direction and race back the other way. As they pounded headlong back up the dark and smelly lane, slippery with refuse, My Li and Tiao could hear more of Han Ying's men coming around the other side of the house to close off their retreat. Once across the gap where the alley opened into the rear lane they had a chance of getting away.

My Li and Tiao almost made it.

Han Ying's men investigated both alleys beside the house. My Li and Tiao's escape depended on them beating their pursuers to where the alley joined the lane, and it became a race to clear it before the Triad men could get there and cut them off. My Li and Tiao reached the gap first but, as they sprinted across it, they were only a metre or two in front of three of the merchant's men running towards them.

The brother and sister might have got away except for the quick thinking of one of their assailants. He was holding a lighted torch and, on seeing the pair in front of him, he hurled it at their running legs.

The heavy torch, spewing burning bits of bitumen and rag, hit My Li heavily behind his calves and became entangled with his striding legs. He crashed to the ground and, still holding Tiao's hand, dragged her down with him. Pulled to their feet by those who had caught them and with assistance from other Han Ying men who had followed the original trio, the youngsters were frog-marched to where the merchant was waiting.

'What a pretty pair! Much prettier than your Mother! She wasn't pretty at all today. Not pretty at all.'

'Where is our mother? What has happened to her?'

'Your mother is dead!' snapped Han Ying.

'The witch tried to cheat me. Well – I'll show her! If I can't have her, I'll have you two. I think I've got the better part of the deal, don't you?'

Neither Tiao or My Li answered him.

'Bring them closer. Hold that torch where it will be of more use! Yes, that's good!' Han Ying had to short-sightedly peer into the torchlight to see them clearly.

He reached out his right arm and tucked Tiao under the chin, forcing her to lift her head so that he could look on her face. 'Come closer girl.'

Tiao did not move and one of Han Ying's armed attendants gave her a shove in her back that pushed her forward, almost on to Han Ying's ample lap. As Tiao regained her composure, Han Ying clutched her arm.

'Why don't you climb in here with me? I realise you won't be as dexterous or as inventive as your mother was trained to be, but I'm sure I can teach you a few tricks, if you're willing – and I'm certain you're going to be willing – otherwise …' Han Ying leant forward toward Tiao, as if he were about to kiss her.

Her upper left arm held firmly by Han Ying's right hand, Tiao lifted her right hand to touch his cheek in what appeared to be a gesture of supplication or endearment. Instead, she dug her finger-nails into Han Ying's face and raked with all her strength. Han Ying shrieked and thrust Tiao away from him.

The power of his heave took his now relaxed attendants by surprise.

First the attendant at the front, left hand corner pole of the sedan-chair staggered, and then the attendant at the front right. Then both simultaneously lost their balance and they tipped Han Ying sprawling onto the street.

As his big but soft body collided with the solid cobbles, the Merchant flung his right arm forward in an attempt to prevent his head striking the street with the full weight of his frame.

By doing so, he saved his skull from cracking like an egg, but caused the ill-fitting ring with the seal of the Triad to slip from his finger and roll towards My Li's feet.

In the pandemonium that followed, My Li, totally unaware of its significance, and with most of the servants' and attendants' attention fixed on their master's predicament, stooped and picked up the ring.

At that moment, the mortified Han Ying, not knowing he had lost the ring, heaved himself to his feet and gingerly touched the raw, bloody grooves down his face. When he felt where his flesh had been opened, saw his own blood on his hand and where it was running freely down his neck and onto his robe, he hissed: 'Kill her!'

My Li could not believe what Han Ying had ordered.

'Nooooo!' cried My Li, and lunged at an armed attendant who drew his sword and took a pace forward. Other servants grasped My Li's arms and restrained him. Someone gripped him savagely by his pigtail. Slipping the seal of the Triad on his finger, My Li used the ring as a knuckleduster and frantically swung his fist in a futile attempt to reach Tiao.

His clenched and now armoured knuckles connected with one of the servants holding him back, and the man's hand loosened. But at that second, the attendant who had chosen to answer his master's order to execute Tiao, a man with a mutilated nose, swung back his blade.

'Run My Li,' cried Tiao, her eyes calm and strangely world weary for one so young.

'Save yourself!'

The sword flashed in the torchlight. Horrified, My Li gaped incredulously as his sister was decapitated before his eyes. A shocked My Li wrenched himself away from the horrendous sight, realising he was not being held. In the moment of horror the servants had forgotten what they were meant to be doing and released their hold on him.

My Li hurled himself out of the circle of light from the torches and ran into the night.

As he ran, he wept.

Ordering his attendants to recapture My Li, Han Ying pressed a handkerchief to the gouges on his cheek. Only then did he notice the ring was missing. 'The ring! I've lost the ring! The seal of the Society. Look for it you fools! All of you. Down on your knees and find the ring!'

Instead of instantly pursuing My Li, the servants and attendants fell to their knees and, grovelling amongst the gravel and dirt stained with Tiao's blood, searched for the seal of the Triad.

The woman known within the lodge of the Black Scarf as the White Fan suddenly appeared at Han Ying's side. 'The ring embodies the authority of the Society. Without the seal our written orders have no legitimacy, and you, our treasurer, will forfeit your life if the ring has been lost.'

The servants groped in vain.

'It isn't here.'

'The youth,' said another. 'I saw him bend. He might have picked it up and taken it with him.'

'I saw a ring in his hand,' someone else said.

'The widow's son!' exclaimed Han Ying, relieved to find there was an extenuating factor reducing his responsibility for the disappearance of the ring.

'The widow's son has stolen the seal. He must be found.'

The White Fan turned to Han Ying. 'Two men should be one too many but we will send two to be sure. Choose quickly …'

Han Ying looked at the attendants silently awaiting further orders.

'Step forward the Red Poles.'

Seven men obeyed and stepped forward. The Master of Ceremonies chose carefully.

'You … and you!' he said, choosing two men, one of which was the recently initiated new recruit. The other was the man with the mutilated nose.

The White Fan spoke so that all could hear her.

'By the authority of the Spirits of our Five Ancestors now vested in me, I allot a task of vengeance. An arm raised against one is raised against all of us. Find the youth and you will find the ring. Kill him – and return with the ring. Go now and prove your worth to the Brotherhood.'

24

The Two Red Poles bowed their acceptance of their task and ran off in the direction My Li was last seen.

Han Ying smiled contemptuously. 'They will be back with his head in an hour or so…'

Overhearing him, the White Fan turned to Han Ying and said coldly, 'For your sake, I hope so, as your behaviour this night has been abominable. And if the Red Poles do not return with the ring you were entrusted with, I will watch you die…'

The White Fan turned on her heel and stalked off into the night, her bodyguards in her wake.

'Vixen!' Han Ying hissed sibilantly when the White Fan was out of earshot.

'You would enjoy that, wouldn't you! You've been waiting for the opportunity to consolidate more power in your hands…'

The Master of Ceremonies stared angrily after the White Fan, then he cast a worried glance after the Red Poles.

'Hurry Up! Don't give her the excuse! Not even the slightest…!'

Han Ying effeminately lifted the hem of his gown and stepped back into his sedan-chair. His servants took deep breaths and hoisted the chair containing its bulky passenger. Stepping over Tiao's headless corpse, his retinue of armed attendants followed the sedan-chair back to the merchant's house.

CHAPTER FOUR

My Li was exhausted. Bitter tears burnt his eyes. He had fled from the village in terror. In the brief respite fate had bestowed on him between Han Ying's orders to find the ring and the despatch of the Red Pole, My Li had managed to cover a kilometre.

At first direction did not matter, distance was everything. But now each abrasive breath brought searing, sharp, stabs of pain to his side. His legs were numb from pounding the roadway and the appalling spectacle of Tiao's gruesome death kept recurring in his brain.

As tiredness took over and his sanity began to return, My Li's pace slackened. The perspiration dried on his body in the cool night air. His instinct for survival was strong and, as his ability to reason was restored, he cut across the paddy-fields that he knew so well from his childhood until he reached the Canton Road.

After an hour and a half of exertion, My Li was staggering. Twice he tripped and fell but managed to regain his feet and keep going. The third time he stumbled, he was unable to recover, and fell headlong into the drainage ditch beside the road. His lungs heaving, My Li lay in the seepage water and slime.

He knew the ditch would be alive with leeches but he didn't care, he had to rest. He lay in the foul mire for some time, listening to his own rasping breath and the croaking of millions of frogs in the surrounding rice paddies. While lying in the muck at the bottom of the ditch, Song Li's words came back to him:

'Unless we do as I've decided, the ditch by the road will become our home...'

Tiao's tear stained face swam before his eyes: 'Even a ditch would be warm if we were together.'

The recollections brought feelings of impotent fury and My Li punched at the mud, coating the heavy ring loose on his finger, with sediment.

My Li had forgotten all about the ring. He stared dumbly at the emblem of the Triad. The embossed characters of the seal burned like a brand in his brain. My Li's first instinct was to throw it as far away as possible, as though it was something dangerously contaminated. Slowly he lowered his arm.

'It will remind me,' he told himself, yet knew he would never need reminding.

Having regained his breath, My Li took stock of his situation. In his flight from the melee and Tiao's murder in the village, My Li had had the presence of mind to cling to his apothecary's satchel. It was with him in the ditch, but the herbs and ointments were individually enclosed in moisture resistant wrappings and would be alright. Nonetheless, he shifted the satchel to ensure water would not saturate it.

Around his waist he wore his father's money-belt that Song Li had presented to him. One of the pockets contained the money that was to pay for his and Tiao's journey to the Great South Land.

He cleaned the grime from the ring and tucked it into an unused compartment in the belt.

My Li was about to haul himself out of the ditch when he became aware of a rhythmic splashing. As first he thought it was a water-buffalo in the nearby paddy-fields but it was too fast, too insistent. He peered over the top of the ditch in time to see the two Red Poles sent by Han Ying and the White Fan – to take back the ring and kill him – climb the bank from the paddy-field and stand quietly panting on the road.

'He couldn't have come this far along the road. By coming across the paddy-fields we have surely cut him off. All we now need to do is head back along the road to the village and we will meet him coming towards us. He will be looking back over his shoulder – expecting trouble from the direction of the village, not from in front of him.'

'Come on then,' replied the other Red Pole, the new recruit the White Fan had named Yung. 'The sooner we catch him the sooner we get home to bed.'

'We had better,' replied the Red Pole with the mutilated nose. 'The other Red Poles will laugh at us for months if we are unable to put an end to one scared kid.'

'The White Fan invoked the sacred phrase. What will she do if we don't find the widow's son?'

'I would rather not find out. Come on. Let's get on with it!'

Every Chinese knew the role the Red Poles played for the Triad so My Li waited until their footsteps faded in the direction of the village before clambering out of the ditch.

He set off at a jog-trot towards Canton.

As the grey tinge of dawn announced a new day that nether Song Li or Tiao would ever see, the two Red Poles returned empty-handed to the village.

Reluctantly, but knowing it was a duty they were unable to avoid, they sought out the merchant Han Ying's house to report the failure of their mission.

The merchant was bleary eyed and irritable from lack of sleep and worry. The new recruit was unable to hide his shame at the unsatisfactory outcome to his first task. The Red Pole revealed nothing of how he felt. His face was a stony mask of indifference. But Han Ying only had to look at their faces, at the new recruit's tired and slumped posture and their mud splattered clothes to immediately know they had not retrieved the ring.

'You idiots,' he fumed through clenched teeth. 'You melon rind suckers! Do you have any idea what this means?'

Determined not to further arouse Han Ying's ill temper, the Red Poles offered no reply.

'What happened?' demanded Han Ying.

The New Recruit blurted out their explanation of what had happened; how they had waded through the paddy-fields to cut off My Li's escape and then, having thought he was trapped between them and the village, how they had returned along the road, checking the ditches and paddy-fields as they walked – but without finding My Li.

'I don't suppose it ever occurred to you that the widow's son might have taken a short cut? You fools! Fools! I'm surrounded by fools!' Han Ying slumped on to a divan.

'There is nothing else I can do,' he said helplessly. 'I will have to inform the White Fan …'

The Merchant clapped his hands twice and a respectful servant appeared. 'Have the sedan-chair brought for me.'

The servant bowed and backed out of the room. Han Ying turned to the two Red Poles. 'You will both come with me. I'm going to see to it that you share whatever fate I suffer!'

The White Fan received Han Ying and the Red Poles in a sparsely furnished room in a house that gave no indication of her position. The only other people present were the White Fan's bodyguards, the Master of the Rolls and the Captain of the Red Poles. The White Fan was not impressed by what Han Ying had to say to her.

'This is a catastrophe for our cause. To be bested by a youth is one thing but, if the seal of the Society falls into the wrong hands, messages contradicting my orders could be sent to our lodge leaders and deeds done in our name that bring us disrepute – even ruin.'

The Merchant and the Red Poles hung their heads. The White Fan waved a hand tipped with long curling nails in exasperation and glowered at the three men pensively awaiting her condemnation.

'I invoked the Sacred Phase in the belief you would have no problem capturing the youth. It was my intention to impress upon those present that there is no escape from the wrath of the Triad. Many present and most of those there heard me use the Sacred Phase and knew of your task. There can be no repudiation of the sacred Phase.'

The Merchant sucked his tongue in apprehension of what might come next.

The White Fan snapped her fingers and the Master of the Rolls – an elderly scholar who held and kept up to date the scrolls containing the names of the Society's members, obediently moved to her side.

'Master of the Rolls,' the White Fan addressed him, 'by the power invested in me by our brethren, I instruct you to take your brush and ink and put a black mark beside these men's names in our rolls.'

The Master of the Rolls bowed. 'What are your names?' he asked Han Ying and the Red Poles.

Han Ying's mouth was so dry he could hardly summon up sufficient saliva to say his name.

The Red Poles, whose original names – those associated with their lives prior to becoming members – were meaningless, gave the names given to them by the Triad.

'My name is Yung,' stated the New Recruit.

'My name is Chang,' said the Red Pole with the mutilated nose.

'Master of Ceremonies ...' said the White Fan.

Han Ying the merchant was praying for leniency and he looked up expectantly.

'... Master of Ceremonies – even though you hold a position of influence within our organisation and also serve as our Treasurer, you are subject to the same rules and laws of the Society as everyone else. Not only did you wake and involve the entire village in your personal life – including myself, when, like many others, I investigated what was going on last night – you have also involved our lodge in your personal affairs. Therefore, I decree the following. These two Red Poles sent to regain the seal of the Triad will be sent forth again. I am told by our informants that the youth and his now dead sister had planned to travel to the Great South Land. I suspect he will hold to his plan.'

Speaking directly to the Red Poles, the White Fan said, 'You will be given money and the names of contacts on the seaboard and overseas. If your pursuit takes you across the sea, then so be it. If you fail in your task, your lives will be forfeit. Further, the Society has decided to impose a time limit on your return. Unless you find the ring and bring it back to this room within eighteen months of this day, our Master of Ceremonies will suffer the Death of One Thousand Cuts ...'

Han Ying swayed on his feet and one of the White Fan's bodyguards caught his arm to support him.

The White Fan continued her decree: 'As Red Poles, you are considered expendable. If you find the ring within the allocated time you will return to glory and promotion. If not, every lodge and member of the brethren will be instructed to hunt you down. There will be no escape for you, either.

Now go, and may the Spirits of our Five Ancestors bless you with success …'

The Two Red Poles bowed. The Master of Ceremonies had to be held up and half carried from the room. The two Red Poles were taken aside by their Captain and issued with more detailed instructions. As they left the room, the White Fan watched them go.

'The four corners of the Earth are now unsafe for the Widow's Son. Mountains and rivers, oceans and deserts will not hide him.'

CHAPTER FOUR

The streets of Canton were crowded, loud humid and polluted with excrement and putrefaction. Pigs provided the city's garbage and refuse disposal. My Li picked his way through the labyrinth of alleys and canopied market stalls that led to the waterfront of Canton harbour.

It had taken him a week to walk the distance from the village and he was weary and hungry. He had avoided hamlets and inns in case someone remembered him and gave information to the pursuers he knew would not be far behind. My Li held no illusions about his fate if he was found. As far as he was concerned, his only chance of obtaining longevity lay with losing himself in the urban sprawl or with the high masted European ships he could see moored beside the wharves. Although he had days ago cleaned the smelly slime of the ditch from his body, he was dust covered and dishevelled, tired and scared. Seeing his first white man did not alleviate his fears.

A party of seamen, heading back to their vessel after a night of whoring, drinking and riotous behaviour, came tottering and clumping down the street, raucously singing as loud as their lungs allowed them.

My Li found them fearsome. They were all huge and hairy and, to My Li, crass.

One seaman stopped and urinated against a wall while his comrades laughed and made obviously lewd gestures. The Chinese watched them sullenly. To object to the white men's behaviour was to invite a beating.

Even the Emperor was unable to tell the white devils to leave China. Not while the cannons of the foreigners' ships were aimed at the commercial hearts of the cities of the seaboard. The Chinese had no military answer to the guns of the Europeans' vessels and were forced to accept the mercenary dictates of the foreigners. They did not, however, have to like what had happened to their country.

It did not take My Li long to find out which was the next ship to leave Canton for the Great South Land. It was named the 'Dayspring', and it was due to leave in two days.

'How do I go about getting aboard?' he asked a coolie working at rebinding an unravelled rope hawser.

'The ship will be towed out on the turn of the tide so to clear the shoals with high water under her hull. Be here the afternoon before she sails. They take the first three hundred people in the queue.'

'Three hundred?'

'That is so. And there will be many more people than space for them. Canton is full of people from the provinces who want to go aboard on the white men's ships. The city is like the basin at the bottom of a fountain. If the fountain spouts water at a rate faster than it can be drained by the pipe that recycles it, then the basin collecting the water will overflow. So it is with Canton.'

My Li thanked the man and turned towards the city.

'And do yourself a favour,' his informant called after him. 'Buy yourself food sufficient for the journey...'

'Why? The fares included food for the voyage?'

The hawser mender spat. 'It does, but from the stories I've heard, it doesn't mean to say you will receive it.'

With time to waste, My Li wandered away from the waterfront. He bought a small bowl of flavoured rice and spent the remainder of the day going from stall to stall and shop to shop, examining a bewildering range of artefacts, foods and services that were unobtainable in the small rural village from where he came.

The sun was beginning to set when he saw a sight that made his blood run cold. Slowly walking side by side down the row of street stalls towards him were two men. Even from a distance of twenty metres or so, My Li recognised the taller of the two. It was the man with the mutilated nose. The man who had killed Tiao.

My Li backed up the street, thanking his ancestors for his good fortune. The setting sun was shining its dazzling late afternoon light directly into the Red Poles' eyes. But as My Li retreated before the approaching assassins, he suddenly saw the street he was in went nowhere. It was a dead end. He had no alternative. Keeping the line of rickety stalls between himself and the Red Poles, he walked to meet them, praying the glare would protect him and that he would be able to slip past without them seeing him.

As the Red Poles approached, they methodically checked out the stalls, their proprietors and the surrounding faces. Their eyes were constantly alert, flicking first to the left and then to the right. My Li felt there was something cold-blooded and reptilian about them. He had just passed a food shop specialising in delicacies such as bear claw soup and monkey's brains, served fresh from the skull, and was almost abreast of the stall where the Red Poles were standing when they saw him.

The stall next to them belonged to a man selling poultry. Some dressed and smoked birds were hanging from the front of his booth and a dozen live brown bantam chickens were on display in bamboo cages.

The Red Pole known as Chang looked at My Li suspiciously but failed to recognise him. The shorter man realised his identity immediately.

'Him! That one there! The one with the satchel!'

The cages containing the chickens were stacked one on top of the other and My Li pushed them in the Red Poles direction and sprinted for the open space at the end of the narrow street. He could hear the chickens squawking behind him and the angry cries of the poultry stall owner as the Red Poles hurled and kicked the fragile cages out of their way, setting two or three of the birds free in the process.My Li had a good start and was able to weave in and out between passers-by, street vendors and carts laden with goods being delivered to the harbour. Without knowing where he was going, My Li led the Red Poles through the back streets with their bordellos, barber shops and bars. But again, unfamiliarity with the layout of the streets found him in yet another dead end. Stopping to catch his breath, he could hear the Red Poles' running footsteps approaching him.

My Li entered a courtyard. The courtyard had doorways on all four sides. My Li had used one doorway. The other three doorways were also wide open. My Li chose the middle door and found himself in a corridor. He quickly walked along it but the corridor did not lead out onto a street. My Li noticed there was an ornate archway half hidden in the dim light at the extreme end of the corridor. He strode to the archway. The archway gave access to an atrium open to the outside air.

The street noises that penetrated to the cool atrium were distant and subdued. Pot plants and shrubs growing in urns and heavy ceramic bowls discreetly placed around the walls, created a pleasant arboreal atmosphere. The floor was tiled in decorative mosaic patterns.

Two doors opened from the atrium. My Li mentally tossed a coin and took the door to his left. The building was worse than the warren of streets outside, My Li thought.

'Well chosen, young man,' said a voice.

Coming out of the bright atrium, My Li blinked and tried to see who owned the voice.

On a small mat against the far brick wall of a bare room sat an elderly Chinese with a wispy, white moustache and a beard that straggled down to his chest. A meal was spread before him on the floor. The old man laughed and beckoned to My Li.

'Don't just stand there. Step forward so I can see you.'

The old man's voice echoed around the atrium. My Li complied. 'They won't find you here. No two men take the same turns in life, and there are many doorways between this room and the outside world.'

My Li glanced over his shoulder.

'Don't be afraid.'

There was a soothing timbre to the old man's voice and My Li decided he was safer inside the building than outside, where the Red Poles would undoubtedly be waiting for him. My Li bowed to show his respect for the elder man.

'A long life and good health to you, sir.'

The old man inclined his head in acknowledgement. 'So far so good. We live as long as we are permitted and get the health we deserve. Sit down young man, I'll strain my neck if I have to keep looking up at you.'

My Li accepted the invitation and sat facing the old man, who affably gestured at the meal between them. 'Join me. Your body is the animal, the horse on which you ride; therefore, treat it well. Please eat. You have ridden your horse hard.'

My Li was still quaking and concerned about the proximity of the Red Poles. The food was frugal – rice, fish, watermelon, lychees and some other fruits with which he was unfamiliar. The old man made small talk and introduced himself: 'My name is Kinqua Liang Lun-Shu but you can call me Kinqua for short'.

My Li began to relax and warm to his host. Before long he was picking at the repast and quietly replying to Kinqua's initially innocent questions.

Finally Kinqua asked: 'From what were you running?'

'Why do you think I was running?'

'Why does rain fall? Why does grass grow? Why do bruised birds seek shelter?'

My Li gazed across to where Kinqua sat, expectantly waiting for his answer, his quizzical young eyes twinkling in a face as lined and crinkled as crumpled paper and My Li let out the pent up emotions associated with the events of the past few days and months. He started the story tentatively but by the time he told Kinqua about the Red Poles hovering somewhere outside, he was talking in torrents of words. Kinqua listened and, when My Li had said everything he wanted to say and talked himself into silence, Kinqua leant forward and, placing a hand on My Li's shoulder, said, 'Take it as an honour that suffering has sought you. It shows that the Lords of Karma think you are worth helping. So be thankful your suffering isn't worse, and that you are alive. Remember the man who thought he was hard done by because he had no sandals but who then met a man who had no feet, and gave grateful thanks for his good fortune. Do you still have the ring?'

'Yes.'

'May I see it?'

My Li hesitated a moment and then showed Kinqua the ring that bore the seal of the Triad. The old man examined the ring intently. He did not simply contemplate the ring. My Li – for an instant – imagined that he was witnessing a clash of wills between the ring and the old man, like two people attempting to out stare each other.

The moment grew into a minute and, to break the spell, My Li cleared his throat. Kinqua looked up as if his mind had been far away. He handed the ring back to My Li, who replaced it in its pocket in the money-belt beneath his shirt.

Outside in the atrium, the sun had set. Crickets chirruped from the shrubs in the pots. Kinqua and My Li sat without speaking in the gloom. Eventually My Li said, 'I don't know how my mother could have done what she did. I am so ashamed.'

'Your mother did what she did out of love for you and your sister,' replied Kinqua. 'You see, men are fathers by chance, woman are mothers by instinct and nature. Where children are concerned, the man is always ruled by his mind; the woman by her heart. It was a noble thing your mother did.'

'Now I am alone,' My Li said resentfully.

'That is true,' said Kinqua. 'Learn now that you are alone in this world, and that no man or woman is your friend or your enemy. They are your teachers. Treat your enemy like a mystery that must be solved. If you solve the riddle that is your enemy, you remove their sting, because you know what they intend before they do it.'

'I don't think I'm capable of that. I don't even know what I should do. Should I go to the Great South Land where I know nobody or should I go somewhere else? I know I can never return to my village, and I know danger has followed me to Canton?'

'Do you still have the money your mother gave you to travel to the Great South Land?'

My Li stiffened and defensively placed a hand on the belt where it rubbed against his skin.

'Yes,' he said doubtfully, wondering what Kinqua's reason might be for asking. Was this the moment the old man's cohorts — who had been waiting for him to reveal his wealth and weakness all this while — would emerge to rob him? But nothing of the kind occurred. Kinqua thought for a minute: 'The South is symbolically associated with justice and magnanimity. I think that is what you should do. I believe it is what your mother would have wished.'

'To continue to the Great South Land?'

'Yes. That is what we will do.'

'We?'

'Yes. I am coming with you. You did say you had enough money for two fares, didn't you?'

'Yes. But don't I have any choice in the matter?'

'Of course. Would you like me to accompany you or not?'

My Li stared at him. 'Yes,' he blurted. 'But why do you want to go? You are too old to dig for gold?'

Kinqua smiled. 'I have a feeling that something important awaits me there. The omens are interesting. Come. I'll show you where you can sleep. Help me up. I've been sitting so long my legs have already gone to bed.'

As Kinqua led My Li out into the atrium, My Li asked: 'What were you doing in there by yourself when I arrived?'

Kinqua's eyes were mysterious. 'Waiting for you of course. Walk on.'

CHAPTER FIVE

.

The following afternoon, My Li and Kinqua were among the first of the three hundred Chinese to file up the Dayspring's gangplank. The rigging and furled sails hung high above their heads. As they reached the deck, gently lifting and dipping under their feet, a surly mate, guarded by two seamen with what My Li and Kinqua thought were clubs but later learnt were belaying pins – used to tie off ropes and occasionally to enforce discipline – collected the payment for their passage. As soon as they had been parted from their money, other European seamen herded the Chinese passengers below, down companion-ways and stairs, cussing and threatening them like cattle until they found themselves in the vessel's dingy and, temporarily, spacious cargo hold.

The ship had been designed to transport bales of wool but had been hastily converted to carry passengers when it was realised how much more money could be made transporting migrants. Four tiers of bunks had been constructed around the walls of the hold. The first passengers into the hold headed straight for the bunks.

'Ignore the bunks,' urged Kinqua rapidly sizing up the situation.

'In hot weather we will suffocate in the bunks.'

'How about over there!' My Li indicated an area under the open hatch.

'Excellent!' said Kinqua. 'But let us be quick. There will barely be room to lie down once everyone is aboard.'

My Li and Kinqua lay claim to floor space at the base of a huge timber beam that rose from the floor to support the main deck above them. They chose well because the beam proved an excellent backrestand, being close to the wooden lattice hatch cover to the hold, they received plenty of fresh air. Kinqua was anxious not to get directly underneath the hatch.

'In rain and rough weather the white men will cover the opening to prevent waves rushing in, but we should still get air,' advised Kinqua.

'And buckets of sea-water probably,' said My Li, experiencing another bout of doubts about going to the Great South Land.

'It is better to be wet and able to breath than to be dry and without breath,' replied Kinqua.

Hundreds of Chinese followed them aboard until the later arrivals began to protest about the lack of room and the air became pungent and oppressive.

My Li was grateful for Kinqua's foresight. Although they were packed half a dozen to a bunk and head to toe with less space between them than herrings in a tin, there was little friction among the men in the hold. The Chinese docilely accepted their confined conditions, a situation Europeans would not have tolerated, and tried to establish a harmonious relationship with whoever was to be their neighbour for the duration of the voyage. Outside, on the wharf, the situation was not so placid. Hundreds of Chinese still hoping to get a berth to the Gold Mountain in the Great South Land were turned away because of lack of available space – which did not occur until there were bodies in the rope-lockers and even parts of the bilge.

They began to howl angrily at the seamen.

Disappointed and knowing they might have to wait weeks for another ship to become available, the rejected Chinese began to quarrel and fight over the final remaining berths. Some, who were rich enough to bribe the seamen, were given preference over the Chinese who could not afford to. Hours passed before the passengers were all below deck.

That evening the Chinese in the hold were given their first taste of the salt beef and hard biscuits that was to become the mainstay of their monotonous diet while at sea. My Li and Kinqua slept fitfully on the floor of the cargo hold, the snores and groans of the cramped humanity around them filled their ears.

The next day, the day of their departure, My Li, Kinqua and the other Chinese were not permitted to watch while the Dayspring winched up its anchor on the squealing capstan, slipped its moorings and was towed into the main channel by sailors at the oars of the vessel's longboat. They would only get in the way they were informed. The few foolhardy Chinese who dared to disobey and attempted to go topside were roughly thrown back into the hold. Guards had been posted to prevent instructions being ignored.

They were, however, told that parties of no more than thirty at a time would be permitted to go up on the main deck to take air and exercise once the ship was at sea.

The Chinese confined to the hold sat silently as the longboat was recovered and hoisted aboard. The deck above resounded to the thump of hurrying feet as the sailors went about their duties. Even in the hold they could feel the tidal current take a grip on the ship. When the sails were finally unfurled and the ship took its propulsion from the wind, a tremor ran the length of the keel, as if the ship's inanimate hulk had been transformed into a living being.

45

The Chinese stared at each other in the dimness; the whites of their eyes wide with apprehension. For most of them, it was their first time on a ship, and the first pitch and roll as the Dayspring encountered the ocean swell filled them with consternation.

A muttering of prayers rippled through the hold. But before long their fears had turned to concerns of a personal kind as their faces turned pale and seasickness overcame them. The stench of vomit filled the hold and My Li instantly felt ill.

As the Dayspring set course for the South China Sea, the man mending rope hawsers, from whom My Li had sought information, was approached by two men. One had a mutilated nose. The men were interested in finding a youth carrying a bag. He was looking for a ship to the Great South Land. They were trying to contact him, they told the rope mender, to inform the youth that his uncle, whom they represented, had died and that he had inherited his uncle's fortune.

The rope mender had a good memory, and he hoped the youth would remember who had sent the messengers of good tidings after him when he became rich and reward him. He told the two men he recalled the youth of their description. He had watched him board the Dayspring the previous afternoon, accompanied by an elderly man.

'Where will we find the ship known as the Dayspring?'

The Rope Mender spat and pointed to the white sails, quickly diminishing in size, among the rusty coloured sails of the junks on the river.

Although the Chinese on the Dayspring did not see the land of their birth recede behind them, they could smell the aromatic mixture of spices, manure and sweat that is the odour of their homeland becoming less distinctive.

Eventually they could only smell the tang of salt and ozone from the open sea.

The Middle – or midnight to dawn –Watch was in charge of the ship by the time My Li and Kinqua's group of thirty Chinese was allowed on deck. Most of them were immediately sick over the side. Kinqua exercised with a Tai Chi sequence, much to the derision of the seamen. My Li simply stared at the waves. He watched them roll away from where the vessel's bow cleaved the sea, mesmerised by the whirling patterns created by the surging rollers and the phosphorescent plankton in the soft light of the sickle quarter moon.

But My Li wasn't seeing the beauty of the sea. In every foam flecked wave, he saw the faces of Song Li and Tiao. Overwhelmed by the sorrow and grief welling up from within him, My Li raised his arms to heaven and cursed those responsible for his sister's death, and the fates that could let someone waste away and die as cruelly as his mother.

My Li cursed the man who had wielded the sword that slew his sister; he cursed the merchant Han Ying; he cursed their families for generations to come and their ancestors long dead; he cursed the cosmos for allowing evil to prosper until, finally, he burst into tears, which he thought were falling for Song Li and Tiao. But they were not. Most of My Li's tears were for himself. The white sailors nearby made derogatory remarks about 'mad Mongols'.

Kinqua waited and watched My Li with eyes that registered infinite sadness. When it was the turn of the next batch of thirty from the hold, Kinqua led My Li below.

'How long will it take the ship to reach Mei-erh-pen?' Kinqua heard one Chinese to another.

'Melbourne? This ship isn't going to Melbourne. Every second voyage it goes to Sydney Town. We are bound for New South Wales. But don't worry. It doesn't matter from where you set out from, it will still be a long, long walk to the Gold Mountain!'

CHAPTER SIX

On the third day at sea, My Li discovered Ah Mouy's brother was with them in the cargo hold. He was travelling with a small contingent from their village. They had left for the coast three days before Song Li had gone to Han Ying's house and knew nothing of what had happened after their departure. Neither My Li or Kinqua mentioned the events that occurred. As My Li was much younger than Ah Mouy's brother and, as he was not friendly with any of his associates, My Li and Kinqua kept their distance.

Despite nothing about My Li's trouble with the Triad being mentioned, My Li suspected that any one of his fellow villagers might be a Triad member and therefore an enemy. My Li spent many hours sullenly staring into a void, deep in depression.

The food offered the Chinese was alien to their diet and the quality deteriorated daily. Dysentery added to their torment. The conditions in the cargo hold became unbearable. The sanitary provisions consisted of an insufficient number of buckets that, when full, were drawn up by ropes through the open hatch and emptied over the gunwales.

If the buckets were already full and the Chinese not permitted on deck, then the contents of the buckets spilled over and soiled the floor of the hold; the same floor men would have to sleep on at night.

The Chinese had also discovered they were to be allowed on deck for as little time as possible. Within a week out of Canton it became apparent that the rule only thirty Chinese were to be on deck at once had more to do the Captain's fear of mutiny over the harsh conditions he forced his paying passengers to endure rather than anything to do with arrangements to facilitate the orderly and smooth running of the ship.

The Captain, whose name was Middleton, and his European crew, seemed determined to treat their Chinese passengers as if they were less than human.

The roster system limiting the number of Chinese on deck instituted by the Captain, meant that My Li and Kinqua were on deck during daylight for one hour every second day. Once the routine for the voyage was established, the Chinese were locked in the hold from midnight till dawn with the hatch battened down. By morning the air was fetid with unwashed bodies and excrement.

It was Kinqua who insisted they should both maintain a rigorous standard of hygiene. It did not matter to Kinqua if the swells were mountainous in height. If they were permitted on deck, then he and My Li went up to cling on the rigging and inhale the clean air. Whenever the weather permitted, he and My Li washed in sea-water collected by tossing a canvas bucket over the side of the hull and hauling it carefully back on board.

Kinqua astonished many who thought he would be too frail to survive the voyage. The first few days were sailed under blue skies and before fair winds, then came the storm that poured a ton or two of sea-water through the improperly secured hatch cover and into the hold.

The canvas cover had only been tied to half its available cleats, and the wind tore it flapping and snapping into the inky and violent night. When the damp and dispirited Chinese morosely welcomed the grey morning light, it was Kinqua who encouraged them and organised them to mop up the surplus water and dry out their bamboo pillows and belongings.

When told that no dry blankets or bedding would be provided, it was Kinqua who made light of the situation by laughing and saying: 'Without bedding we will have fewer lice.'

When the weather turned sultry and sticky, the Chinese condemned to the stinking hold suffered from heat exhaustion. Some began to hyperventilate and Kinqua had them brought from the bunks, where they had tried to make them comfortable on the open floor under the hatch, where they received the occasional breath of air.

'At least we will sleep warm,' quipped Kinqua.

It was Kinqua who suggested they should play games to pass the time.

'What with?'

Kinqua learnt that a man from Szechwan had a ping pong ball and before long he had organised a tournament without bats or tables. It was played by striking the ball with the open palm of their hands. A game of volley ball was played under the open hatch with spare clothing bundled into a ball. By day, the non-players shuffled aside to give space to the competitors. At night the playing field was reclaimed by sleepers.

When the beef and biscuits offered to them were seen to be rotten and alive with maggots and weevils, Kinqua purchased fishing lines and hooks from the sailors and obtained permission for the Chinese to fish over the side to supplement their diet. Permission was granted so long as only thirty men were on deck simultaneously. Kinqua reconciled the order with their need for fish by organising that the fishing lines stayed constantly on deck while the hands holding them changed.

Whereas Kinqua started each day with a callisthenics class, which he led by example and appeared to grow in strength and fortitude as their living conditions deteriorated, others wilted, including My Li.

Forewarned by the rope mender on the dock at Canton, Kinqua and My Li had bought a small stock of dried foods which Kinqua doled out to those in need. With a borrowed clear glass bottle and bean sprout seeds bought before departing, Kinqua and My Li were able to sustain their essential vitamin intake.

Ah Mouy's brother was among the most ill and disillusioned.

'You must not allow yourself to become negative, chided Kinqua, 'You will infect others and make their lives harder, which you have no right to do.'

But the sea-water that had poured into the hold when the storm tore away the canvas hatch cover had also found its way into other parts of the ship. Unknown to either the crew or passengers, the bulk of their drinking water was brackish and unfit for human consumption, and all of Kinqua's kind words and wisdom could not alleviate the reality of their plight. After a month at sea, with hundreds of Chinese weakened and suffering from a variety of illnesses, death stalked them.

The first deaths amongst the Chinese brought the friction between the European crew and their passengers to a spark that threatened to become incendiary, for the crew threw the corpses overboard without rites or funerals. The Chinese were extremely offended. A proper funeral was their key to a blissful, eternal afterlife. Without a funeral their souls would be damned and denied entrance to

Heaven; condemned to be unsatisfied souls inhabiting a half-world of shadows and shades, forever in limbo between Heaven and Earth. To the Chinese, the crew's behaviour exhibited a callous disregard of propriety; an insult of great magnitude.

The Christian crew was likewise dismayed by the sight of the Chinese tossing dice for possession of the meagre belongings of the dead. The white men saw such incidents as indicative of a pagan lack of respect for the deceased.

When the seamen came to collect yet another body, one of the Chinese held them at bay with a knife. Reinforcements arrived at the scene and the Chinese was disarmed. The angered sailors were about to heave the struggling Chinese who had confronted them overboard when a young midshipman intervened. Kinqua was able to make him realise the Chinese were not being mutinous but merely concerned for the tranquillity of their souls.

The Midshipman obtained permission for the Chinese to hold short funeral services before the bodies were consigned to the deep.

In an attempt to prevent the disease, whatever it was, spreading to the crew, the white seamen refused to allow the Chinese out of the hold and battened down the hatch, even during daylight hours.

Until the passengers began dying, My Li had remained absorbed in his private anguish.

'You must help! It is your duty,' pleaded Kinqua.

'Duty? What duty? I have no obligation to anyone other than myself!'

'That is exactly what I am getting at,' replied Kinqua. 'You are trained to alleviate suffering. More than anyone here you could help ease the agony of those in pain!'

'Why should I? I didn't see anybody raise any objections when Tiao had her head chopped off! None of our neighbours bothered to offer Song Li help when she

53

was trying to raise two children by herself. No! She was different – an ex-courtesan! And everyone knows no self-respecting citizen should be seen talking to a tainted ex-courtesan. Yet those same self-satisfied citizens probably paid protection money to the Triad! I'm sorry Kinqua, I don't believe I have any 'duty' to other people, as you put it. It would be hypocritical of me if I did.'

Kinqua looked at My Li in anguish. 'Then tell me what to do and allow me the use of the contents of your apothecary bag.'

'Help yourself,' replied My Li. 'But don't lecture me about 'duty'!'

For days Kinqua shuffled between the seriously ill and where My Li sat propped against the beam, staring forlornly at the rays of daylight that penetrated the cracks in the deck and where the repaired hatch cover was stitched and sewn. Kinqua would relate the patient's symptoms to My Li, who invariably would answer disinterestedly, 'cover your thumb-nail with granules from the container with the picture of the dragon's head on it and administer it to the man' – or give whatever other instruction was necessary.

Kinqua cunningly kept returning to My Li for more instructions. 'The man with the granules from the tin with the dragon's head on it – he's been retching but has fallen asleep. He seems comfortable now.'

'That's good. The medicine has done its work. His fever has broken. He should recover.'

For Kinqua, the breakthrough came when Ah Mouy's brother took a turn for the worse.

'He's asking for you. He wants to give you a message for his family in case he does not survive.'

'He can tell it to his friends.'

'He wants to entrust it to you too. He says you have a greater chance of returning to your village one day because you are younger.'

My Li sighed. 'If it makes him happier, I'll listen to his message – but I'll never be returning to that village.'

When he came to Ah Mouy's brother, he found he was sharing a bunk with four others and sweating copiously. My Li lifted his eyelids and took note that his pupils were dilated. After feeling for his pulse, My Li said, 'cholera.'

The dreaded word passed from mouth to mouth throughout the ship.

After politely listening to Ah Mouy's brother's message for his family, My Li visited all the sick to determine the extent of the disease. Some were simply suffering from common virus infections; some were feeling the effects of dysentery but there were sixteen men showing symptoms associated with cholera. The Chinese formed a council to discuss what to do. A rebellion to take over the vessel was out of the question. There were no deep water sailors among them. There were some men who had handled junks on the Yellow River but no-one who might have taken over the navigation of the ship. Besides, since the Chinese objected to the bodies of their country men being thrown to the sharks, the European sailors had begun going about armed with pistols and cutlasses.

The council asked My Li's advice. He shrugged his shoulders. 'Keep the cholera victims separate from those who are healthy. Find a clean source of fresh water. Improve our sanitary conditions and food.'

The council and all the other Chinese were well aware My Li's requirements for improved health were impossible.

Kinqua solved one problem for My Li and himself by collecting rain-water that dripped through the hatch cover whenever the Dayspring encountered squalls. It was impractical to attempt to collect the rain-water for the other Chinese. They had to continue using the contaminated water supply. One of the Chinese discovered the crew had confiscated the least affected barrels for there own use.

Late one night, My Li was roused from his sleep. His name was being called. Three sailors wanted him to accompany them. My Li was frightened. One of the members of the Chinese council approached: 'They want you to examine one of their kind. They have heard you are treating the sick and saving some from certain death. We beg you to go with them. If you can help, then we will be able to negotiate from a stronger position. For the sake of your brethren…'

My Li was taken to the poop deck where the officers were quartered. He sucked in the cool, clean air and wished he could take some back for Kinqua. One of the seaman knocked deferentially on a door. The door swung open and My Li stood in the yellow glow of the lamp lit interior. An officer in a braided jacket with brass buttons brusquely indicated My Li should enter.

My Li did as he was requested. The officer stood at the far end of the cabin, his back to the wall. On a bunk to one side sat two other young officers, concern obvious on their faces. Against the opposite wall was another bunk, in which lay a young European. He was without clothes and his perspiring pale body was covered only by a sheet. My Li immediately recognised him as the midshipman who had prevented the Chinese who had defending their dead from being tossed overboard, and obtained permission for funeral services from the Captain.

One of My Li's seaman escort spoke understandable basic Chinese and acted as interpreter. My Li did not require an interpreter to comprehend what was required of him. The midshipman was gravely ill and the officers wanted to know if the cholera had reached their own kind. My Li took his time until more than satisfied in his own mind.

'It isn't a problem. It is the disease you call smallpox.'

'Can you help him,?'

'Perhaps.'

'Do you think the disease can be kept to this man only? The Captain says he his short-handed as it is and requires every able-bodied man to work the ship.'

'It is possible – perhaps.'

'Captain Middleton says he will reward you if you can save the boy's life. The midshipman is a relation by marriage.'

'Would the Captain agree to opening the hatch and letting good air into the hold?'

My Li waited while the translator turned his words into English. Captain Middleton was a podgy man with a prominent nose and thick lips. The Captain kept his eyes fixed on My Li as the interpreter translated.

'Yes!' he snapped.

Emboldened, My Li tried to press home his advantage. 'We need to empty the slop buckets twice a day while there is so much illness, and if we clean and replenish the water barrels when it next rains, we might be able to contain the disease …'

The seaman translated again, and then gave My Li the Captain's reply. 'The Captain says save the boy first and you have a bargain.'

My Li stayed with the midshipman for forty-eight hours, hardly leaving his side for a second. First he tied the midshipman's arms to his bunk to prevent him scratching his sores and causing himself scars. Then he mixed a medicinal draught from the apothecary's dispensary in his bag and patiently coaxed the midshipman to swallow it. The patient passed into a drug induced sleep and, as My Li's medicine began to work, My Li washed and wiped the midshipman's body with cool compresses and strove to reduce his temperature.

By the time My Li left the cabin, the midshipman was smiling at him in gratitude and sharing comments with the officers who periodically visited him to encourage his recovery.

Back in the cargo hold, My Li told the Chinese of his deal with Captain Middleton. When the ship next encountered rain, the Captain ordered the cleaning and the replenishment of the water barrels. The Chinese were also permitted to empty the excrement buckets twice a day and the hatch was uncovered during daylight. The quality of their food, however, did not improve. Nor were the Chinese allowed on deck again. By the time they saw their first land bird through the lattice grill of the open hatch and heard the look-out cry 'Land ho' from the top of the main mast, thirty-six Chinese had died and six more would not see the new land.

Ah Mouy's brother was one of those buried at sea.

CHAPTER SEVEN

Avessel flying the yellow and black flags signifying disease and death were among its passengers could not be authorised to enter a British harbour. Passengers aboard European ships who found they had contracted contagious diseases, were quarantined ashore to prevent an epidemic.

The quarantine station at Sydney was located at the North Head, on the opposite side of the harbour and miles away from the settlement.

But the Dayspring was carrying Oriental passengers, and was consequently instructed by the maritime authority to wait at sea, off the heads of Port Jackson, for a period of several weeks until the disease had run its course and abated. When emptying the slop buckets, the lucky Chinese entrusted with the chore could see the distant cliffs of the shoreline shimmering beneath the brown smudge of smoke from domestic and bush fires. The smoke had a faint eucalyptus odour from the burnt gum trees that fuelled the fires.

When ships were prohibited from entering the harbour by the quarantine laws, it was customary for fresh vegetables and meat to be ferried out to a quarantined ship and transferred at the owners' expense until compensation could be claimed from the passengers.

Captain Middleton was only too aware that most of his passengers' capital was already locked in the Dayspring's safe. Captain Middleton was impatient. Besides being in personal danger from the disease still rampant on board, he was also losing money daily due to the delay in the ship's turn around time for the pre-arranged return trip to China with a load of fine merino wool.

As he was an unscrupulous man who saw his Chinese passengers as less than human, and the health of the colony as nothing to do with him, he decided, contrary to the harbour authority's instructions, to put his passengers ashore so that he could get on with recouping his costs.

A ship's provender aboard the yawl that delivered supplies to the Dayspring was paid to take a letter, sealed with red wax, ashore. Four days later, a reply addressed to Captain Middleton was brought out to the ship.

After nightfall the next day, with only constellations to steer by, the Dayspring raised anchor and sailed southwards along the coast past Botany Bay. The wind was an unseasonal and gusty northerly, and they made good speed. By noon the next day the Dayspring had dropped anchor once more, this time off a beach between two rocky headlands.

A metre high surf surged and frothed towards the sand. Tree covered hills and a sandstone escarpment sloped to the beach and, when the surviving Chinese were brought up on deck, the smell of the wattle trees in bloom struck their olfactory senses like a dose of smelling salts. After their lengthy incarceration, the glare of the sunlight hurt their eyes. Their bodies were emaciated by malnutrition and disease.

As the Dayspring's longboat and dinghies were lowered into the sea, the Chinese assumed their ordeal was over and excitedly talked and laughed amongst themselves.

Jacob's ladders – rope ladders with wooden rungs – were dropped down the hull and the Chinese were ordered into the boats. Their elation turned to consternation as they realised they would have to negotiate the ladders and pounding surf in their frail and weakened physical state.

A fearful hush fell over them.

The silence was broken by Captain Middleton. 'Break out the cat-o'-nine-tails Mr. Mate. That will soon get them moving.'

The mate complied, and the mere sight of the whip, with its dozens of knots and flesh tearing lumps of lead crimped to the ends of the leather thongs, was sufficient inducement to send the suddenly dejected Chinese over the side of the ship.

As only a dozen could cram into a boat at a time, the others stoically waited on the deck of the Dayspring. The longboat led the less seaworthy dinghies towards the shore. As the laden boats reached the outermost white water and wallowed on the heavy swell, the boatmen in command ordered their Chinese passengers to leap into the surf.

To the Chinese, the unfamiliar surf was terrifying and the water too deep to wade to shore.

'Go on! Jump! We're not a cab service!'

The reluctant Chinese cowered and stared in alarm at the breakers crashing on to, and washing up, the beach.

'Jump damn you! The boats could get wrecked if we take them too close to shore!' a boatman shouted, and he threatened his passengers with a belaying pin.

They had no option. The Chinese resigned themselves to their fate and lowered themselves or leapt, plunged and dived into the water. Those who refused to leave the boat were cudgelled with belaying pins and beaten with oars, until, bleeding and desperate to escape, they hurled themselves into the sea. Chinese knocked unconscious by the blows were thrown after their comrades.

Watching from the Dayspring, My Li and Kinqua were horrified to see some of their countrymen were calling desperately for assistance. Most of the men were from inland provinces and could not swim.

All of the Chinese were debilitated from the effects of the voyage and only a few were strong enough to support someone else in the water. The most fortunate were those picked up by a surging wave and tumbled, arms and legs flailing, onto the safety of the sand.

Those that made it to the beach had another surprise in store for them.

My Li and Kinqua were in the second wave of boats to the beach. Unlike those in the earlier wave, most of the Chinese in the boats did not need to be beaten before leaping into the surf. My Li was concerned with keeping his apothecary's satchel out of the water and how to prevent Kinqua from drowning.

'I can't swim,' Kinqua had informed My Li as they climbed down the Jacob's ladder to the dinghies.

In the boat, My Li had passed his satchel to Kinqua.

'Here! Hold this for me – and whatever you do, don't let go of it.

'Its weight will take me to the bottom and lessen my suffering. Thank you My Li. It is kind of you to consider me…'

'Don't be stupid Kinqua! I have no intention of letting you drown. I learnt to swim in the irrigation canals at home, so if you hold onto the bag and keep holding your breath, I'll be able to tow you to shore.'

When the time came to jump into the sea, My Li leapt in first. 'Pass me the satchel! I'll hold it till you are in the water.'

The bag passed between them again and Kinqua slid over the bow of the dinghy and held onto the prow while My Li positioned himself behind him.

My Li trod water and gripped the old man by the pigtail that hung to his buttocks.

'Now you take the satchel.'

The bag changed hands again and, while Kinqua floated on his back, puffing and spluttering like a surfacing whale, My Li swam side-stroke and tugged Kinqua through the waves until his feet touched the bottom. Once his feet felt firmness underfoot, My Li was able to support, half carrying and half dragging his elderly companion, onto the beach. They collapsed and lay side by side, unable to speak but grinning widely at one another.

As their breathing returned to normal they sat up and looked back out to sea. The boats had already returned to the ship and another group of Chinese was descending the ladders. Closer to shore, bodies that made no attempt to reach the beach floated face down in the waves. Behind them, on the wet sand where the surf met the land, other inert figures were lapped by the sea.

My Li staggered to his feet. He was about to investigate whether one of the nearby bodies had any hope of life when he stopped still in his tracks. Preoccupied with the process of getting ashore, he had not noticed there was a reception committee waiting for the waterlogged Chinese dragging themselves onto the beach.

In the shade of the tree-line sat a dozen Europeans on horseback. They were cleanly dressed in dark fabrics that seemed too heavy and beards too hot for the climate. They were also armed with pistols and what My Li assumed to be muskets but which were in fact more modern rifles. Another half dozen Europeans were scattered, sitting and lying on their backs, under the enormously wide, white trunked gum trees.

On closer inspection, My Li saw they too were cradling firearms, and then he realised they were guarding the first group of Chinese to come ashore, who were squatting on their heels recovering from their ordeal. My Li, Kinqua, and the other Chinese with them who had survived the surf, had no choice but to join them.

Nothing was said until the last of the passengers from the ship stumbled up the beach. Over two hundred wet, bedraggled and ill Chinese were gathered on antipodean soil. When the entire party was reunited, the Europeans who had been lazily guarding them, swung into their saddles. Then the white men who had stayed on their mounts the entire time the landing was taking place, nudged their horses out from under the trees. They advanced at a walk until only a few metres away from where the Chinese sat.

To the amazement of the Dayspring's passengers, one of the Europeans addressed them in Cantonese dialect. 'Welcome to the Great South Land, brothers.'

As every eye swivelled in his direction, the Chinese saw that beneath the man's western garments, he was an oriental like themselves.

Grieved at their recent treatment, and with the bodies of their shipmates who did not make it to the beach still bobbing in the water behind them, the Chinese did not respond. The oriental wearing white men's clothes was unperturbed.

He grinned and went on: 'I am Wei Tzu-san. The white men call me Wee San. I have been here ten years. My master's name is Mr. MacArthur. He is the man on the chestnut gelding. He is a rich man, and so are his friends, Mr. Wentworth, the man to his right and Mr. Thomas Braidwood, to his left. That is Mr. Blaxland over there by the big rock. These men are now your masters too. For you are each indentured to one of them for one year.'

The Chinese stared in disbelief at the grim faced Europeans and a ripple of discontent ran among them.

'But we are free men! We paid for our passage,' cried one. 'You can't do this to us!'

Wei Tazu-san, or Wee San the interpreter spoke again. 'Captain Middleton has sold your debt to him to Mr. MacArthur and his friends. Now divide into four equal groups. You are going to go to different places.'

'But this is not right,' retorted another Chinese. 'We do not owe Captain Middleton. If anything he owes us. He reneged on providing us food for the voyage. He mistreated us ...'

'Enough,' snapped Wee San abruptly. His genial mood of only moments earlier disappeared. 'According to my masters, you all owe Captain Middleton for food you consumed over the weeks while in quarantine waiting to enter harbour. Captain Middleton has taken a great risk in getting you ashore. If the authorities find out you are here, you will all be returned to China for evading the quarantine regulations.'

'But we were forced ashore!'

'Captain Middleton has already told my master you illegally jumped ship without his consent. Do you want to be handed over to the government?'

The Chinese were stunned. From their experiences with the imperial regime in China, being handed over to the government would almost certainly result in their deaths or at least labouring for life as slaves. They were probably better off being indentured for a year to these foreign devils, most of them thought. After that time expired, they would be free to seek the Gold Mountain they had risked all to find.

One man, unbalanced from his privations, disagreed. 'Curse you!' screamed a Chinese on the side of the throng nearest the trees. 'I haven't come this far and gone through all this to work for some heathen! I'm going to the gold-fields! And nobody is going to stop me!'

Having made his statement, the Chinese determinedly strode inland. Wee San watched him go, motionless on his horse. When the shot rang out, Wee San had to stroke his animal's neck to calm it. Some of the other horses whinnied and would have bolted except for the firm hands of their riders. The Chinese who had decided to go his own way was lying still on the ground with blood staining his light cotton blouse.

My Li did not need a closer look to know the man would not move again.

'Those who cannot pay the Government's Entrance Tax will be indentured for two years not one,' announced Wee San. A European calmly reloaded his rifle.

The Chinese were given consent to bury their dead and then told to divide into four parties as instructed. They then shuffled off with either Mr. MacArthur, Mr. Blaxland, Mr. Braidwood or Mr. Wentworth at their head. The other Europeans were their employees and they accompanied each party as armed guards. My Li and Kinqua found themselves walking in the dust behind Mr. MacArthur.

'What can we do?' My Li asked Kinqua.

'Walk on,' said the old man, smiling, 'We are alive!'

CHAPTER EIGHT

Like a tired and bedraggled caterpillar, the human cargo of the Dayspring filed their weary way through the peaceful Australian bush. Yellow eyed currawongs and kookaburras bemusedly looked down on what appeared from afar to be a strange giant creature creeping over the landscape.

The kookaburras occasionally broke into cackling laughter at their appearance and laboriously slow progress. The further the insect-like procession wormed through the scrub, the smaller it became, as one party and then another split off from the main body and went their own way. The first to go was Wentworth's party. They were followed by Blaxland and, when Braidwood, shook hands with MacArthur and led his band off to the south west, MacArthur's party went on alone.

The Chinese with MacArthur were a week on the track. To begin with, like a Chinese chain-gang, they tramped disconsolately after the string of pack horses that carried the maize meal they were given to eat, and which they mixed and heated into a tasty gruel. Although all of the Chinese were thin and many were still laid low from the effects of disease and their previous experiences, being on dry land with clean air, sunshine, exercise and reasonably wholesome food had an enervating, uplifting effect on their spirits.

My Li and Kinqua experienced their first encounter with camping outdoors, Australian style. When they stopped in the evening, fires were lit and the Chinese prepared their gruel.

The white men kept themselves apart and prepared damper – a cake of flour and water without a raising agent – and brewed black tea. The Chinese were also given tea and, when the Europeans had eaten their fill, the left over damper – or extra loaves cooked for the purpose – were handed to them. Food did not appear to be in short supply.

There was no-one who was seriously ill among the Chinese to slow their advance – they had already died; and the pace MacArthur set for them was considerate. There was a general shortage of working men in the colonies and MacArthur had no intention of losing any of the cheap labour he had coerced into his employ. By the time they reached MacArthur's sheep-run, the fifty Chinese left were feeling decidedly stronger than when they set out. They marched across the sheep-grazed grass plain towards the cluster of buildings that was to become home, for many years for some of them. The white workers, cooks, rouseabouts, stable-hands and domestic servants emerged to watch their arrival.

Most of the Chinese were still wearing the traditional blue or white padded blouses that reached to their thighs, in which they had left Canton. Some had discarded their heavier garments when struggling ashore and now only wore their loose cotton undershorts and baggy trousers, tied below their knees. A few had retained their slippers with pointed turned up toes or wore sandals. Many were barefooted. All of them had shaved heads, except at the back of their skulls where their hair had been plaited into long pigtails, often with ribbons to hold them in place — a practice continued even in the hold of the Dayspring.

With their Asiatic features and rapid foreign speech, they might well have come from another planet as far as the Europeans were concerned, not merely another country.

The Chinese slowed as they approached.

In the middle of the vast emptiness through which they had spent days walking without seeing another human being, was a tiny outpost of civilisation; made to appear even less significant than it was by the enormity of the Australian wilderness that surrounded it.

The sheep-run was a self-contained township that largely provided for itself – apart from regular but few and far between bullock dray loads of supplies they were unable to manufacture themselves.

The main homestead had been built from the easy to cut outcrops of yellowy orange sandstone ubiquitous to the region. It had a wood-shingled roof that extended out from the building to create a wide, shady verandah stretching the length of each of the dwelling's four walls, held up at its extremities by stout timber poles. A kitchen constructed from iron bark stood to the rear of the homestead. Its sandstone chimney belched smoke into the otherwise clear, blue sky. A cold store and pantry, similarly built from hewn stone, was to one side of the cookhouse. The space between the three solid buildings formed a courtyard cooled by a shadow from one of the structures no matter what time of the day. There was a little other shade.

A hundred metres from the buildings was a large sheep yard made from wooden rails. A big shed with a timber floor raised off the ground, sides open to the elements and a roof of over-laid bark was on the far side of the sheep yard. My Li and Kinqua were soon to learn this was the shearing and woolshed. Beyond the shearing-shed were a dozen huts with timber slab walls – some caulked and daubed – packed dirt floors, and roofs comprised of strips of bark peeled from trees, to keep out rain.

Trimmed branches and large rocks had been lifted up onto the bark to hold it in place during high winds.

Several white men, their hands in their trouser pockets and their expressions sour and resentful, morosely stared at the arriving Chinese from in front of the shearing-shed. One of them stooped, picked up a stone lying on the ground, straightened and threw it at the Chinese. Another man followed his example. Their friends encouraged them with hoots and jeers of derision.

'Go on Harry, give it to the bastards!'

The stone struck one of the Chinese in the arm.

'Well aimed Harry!'

'Go back to where you came from, you bloody Chinks!'

MacArthur spurred his horse forward and interposed himself between the aggressive whites and the Chinese. 'Stop it!' he roared. 'Stop I say! I'll have order if you please!'

The white men were young and MacArthur was a landowner and a man of authority in the colony. They did as they were told. A rock about to be hurled was dropped. The young men kicked the toes of their boots into the ground.

MacArthur walked his horse towards the offending young men. 'Last year and the year before, you washed my sheep at a reasonable price. But this year you tripled your fees knowing most of the able-bodied men in the district have gone to the diggings. You thought you had me over a barrel and that I would have to accede to your usurious demands. Well, I've got news for you! I'm not made of money and I will not have any man use stand-over tactics to dictate to me! I'm going to use these Mongols to do your jobs and I'll only pay them a fraction of what you were greedily trying to get out of me. So, as of this moment, you are no longer working for me – you are out of work! Now clear off or I'll have my men kick you off the property!'

'You'll grow a pigtail next, MacArthur!'

'Scum! that's what they are! They'll work for the smell of an oily rag!'

'This country should be kept white!'

MacArthur turned to his armed men.

'Take the Chinks to the cookhouse and make sure they are well fed. I don't want to see any of these hotheads around here after I have finished my lunch.'

With the aplomb of a man used to giving orders and having his instructions complied with, MacArthur rode over to the homestead, dismounted and stalked inside.

The redundant sheep-washers dispersed to collect their belongings.

That night, in the shearing-shed where the majority of the Chinese had been billeted, the bark roof reverberated with their snores. Unable to sleep, My Li stared into the darkness. Kinqua lay dozing by his side.

'Kinqua,' whispered My Li.

There was no reply.

'Kinqua,' My Li's voice was more urgent.

Kinqua opened his eyes. 'What is the matter? Is something wrong?'

'What will become of us, Kinqua? I am young and foolish while you are old and wise; is life simply one misery followed by another?'

'If you allow it to become so.'

'Allow it? So far I haven't had any choice!'

'Go to sleep My Li. That man MacArthur will want his money's worth from us in the morning. We must have eaten half of his flock tonight.'

'I can't. I'm too tired.'

'Your voice has a whine in it that is beginning to sound to me like the droning of a bee in an empty room. If I tell you a story will you go to sleep?'

'Your stories always put me to sleep.'

'Then listen carefully. A mean man owned a cart and a donkey to pull it. The donkey knew that when there was a road, he walked along it. When the man said *whoa*, the donkey knew he should stop, and when he said *hike*, the donkey knew he should go backwards. When the man said *yup*, the donkey knew to go forward again. That was the donkey's life. If the donkey questioned its commands, it was hit with a stick or boot or lump of rock but if he went along with his instructions, he was never hit. And that, to the donkey, was happiness. Do you see my point My Li? My Li?'

But My Li did not answer. My Li was sound asleep.

CHAPTER NINE

In the morning, the fifty Chinese who awoke under the roof of the MacArthur's shearing-shed were divided again — this time into three contingents. Two parties were sent to work on neighbouring leases. The third party was given breakfast and then taught how to wash sheep. My Li and Kinqua were with the Chinese who remained at the MacArthur homestead.

For Kinqua and My Li, life almost became settled and sedate for a while. The tasks they were allocated included hoeing and weeding the vegetable garden near the creek that provided the sheep-station with its water supply; pruning the grape vines; harvesting the grain crops; threshing, grinding, fencing and the never ending demands of looking after the thousands upon thousands of sheep that roamed the property. The MacArthur flock was organised in several mobs, and the mobs were moved around the countryside in such a way they did not have to graze where other sheep had already passed. The sheep-herders guarded them against wild dingo dogs, foraging Aborigines, foot-rot, catarrh and scabby mouth, which could rapidly infect the entire flock.

My Li and Kinqua learnt how to treat what was usually a fatal disease, as they had to justify and explain the death of every sheep while they were in charge of them. If sheep were lost through negligence, the culprits were flogged in front of their countrymen.

The work was not pleasant. The sheep attracted blowflies and infections of maggots that had to be cut from their wool and their skin. The sheep were then bled and bathed in heady mixtures of turps, tobacco and water. My Li and Kinqua learnt how to castrate and butcher the beasts.

The washing of the sheep took place before the shearing. With the assistance of trained dogs, the animals were rounded up and driven into the creek, which was the reason for the sheep-run's location. For days the sheep were made to swim in and out and up and down the stream. And then, and then only, did the washing start. Men had to lather the fleeces with soap to remove the grease before passing the animals to others who scoured the wool. They then forced the animals to swim upstream to rinse it.

Depending on the kind of food, and the disposition of the cook, the Chinese would frequently collect their meals at the kitchen and eat nearby. On other occasions they received rations of rice, millet, dried fruit, mutton and bread, taking them back to the huts and woolshed, that had become their homes, and cook their food themselves over open fires. Sometimes the kitchen staff made soup, and delegations of Chinese would be sent to collect and carry the vats back to the huts and the woolshed. As he was one of the youngest and most diligent of the Chinese, My Li was often asked to collect rations or vats for his elders.

His trips to the kitchen brought him into contact with a girl who worked in its hot interior. Her mother was employed as a dishwasher and lackey to the cook, helping with the preparation of meals destined for the homestead's dining table. The mother was a coarse woman who constantly ill-treated her daughter. In the evenings, she dropped her underwear behind the cold store for any of the white workers prepared to pay for the privilege. If anything within the woman's realm of responsibility in the kitchen went wrong, or if a dish was accidently shattered, then it was the daughter's fault and never that of the mother.

The girl's father was also employed by MacArthur. He was the blacksmith, the only one within a hundred miles, and neighbours brought their broken and bent farm implements to the MacArthur's forge to be fixed. He also was in charge of the armoury and, when not busy at his trade, was used by MacArthur as a bodyguard and bully to enforce his will.

The blacksmith was more bestial then the beasts he served. Too dumb to be cruel, he was brutal to human beings and beasts alike. He always pocketed the coins his wife earned from her overtime behind the cold store. If his wife attempted to hide her extra income from him, he would beat her until she handed the proceeds over. The blacksmith made no secret of the fact he despised the Chinese, and My Li, sensing his explosive and intolerant character, avoided having to deal with him if at all possible.

The daughter was an enigma to both their natures.

She suffered the blows she received, mainly from her mother, without retaliation and without cringing. Whenever the mother lost her temper, the girl remained passive. When she worked, she worked hard enough for two and her lazy mother was able to pretend she worked harder than she did. When free from her work, which was a rarity, she liked to roam the paddocks around the homestead. She rarely spoke and, if she did, it was usually to one of the livestock, to whom she had given individual names.

The girl's sole joy seemed to be in bringing back lizards or injured birds and animals, such as flying foxes and possums, which she delighted in nursing back to health. The white workers thought the girl was imbecilic and, in the unmerciful and ignorant manner of the time, treated her harshly. Her name was Simone, so they called her 'Simple Simone'.

One day, about six months after My Li and Kinqua had arrived at the MacArthurs, they were part of a team of Chinese assisting the blacksmith repair the axle to the dray.

The shaft had been bent whilst drawing a heavy load of rocks and gravel to replace washed away gravel at the creek ford. The blacksmith had spent the morning sweating over the anvil, alternatively beating and pounding the axle until it was straight again.

He was tired and irritable and, when Simone, who had been feeding a galah whose broken wing she had splinted, was slow in fetching him the cold drink he ordered her to bring him, he sent the rising girl flying with a backhanded blow and stamped the life out of the bird. The girl quickly bounced to her feet and brought her father the water.

It was the only time My Li ever saw Kinqua become genuinely angry, and he had to restrain the old man from saying or doing something they both might regret.

'No Kinqua. It will be of no use,' My Li said softy and held Kinqua by his wrist.

'Know this,' Kinqua later said to My Li, '...the karma of cruelty is the most common of all. It is done in the name of religion; it is done in the name of lust; of thoughtlessness and greed. Many school teachers do it habitually. Learn to recognise it in the heart of men so that you understand the world in which you live.'

Worse occurred one morning when My Li was a member of the brigade collecting the breakfast ration. He was waiting outside the door to the kitchen with the others sent to bring back the rations to where the Chinese were already at work, clearing scrub, kilometres from the homestead. The waiting Chinese could see through the door inside the kitchen. Simone's mother was in an especially vile mood, hectoring and scolding her daughter over trivial and silly things. But, for once, Simone seemed unable to cope as well as usual.

Her mother was boiling eggs for the MacArthurs. She told Simone to bring her a tray already set with egg-cups and toast in a rack. Her mother intended to ladle the eggs out of the saucepan on the stove and onto the tray.

Simone did as she was bid but in her haste to appease her mother, tilted the tray causing one of the egg-cups to fall to the floor and smash. Her mother lost her temper and slapped Simone, who was still holding the tray, across her face. Forgetting about the tray, Simone raised her hands to protect her face from her mother's anger, and the tray followed the egg-cup to the floor.

Simone's mother went berserk. In her hand was a saucepan filled with boiling water and eggs. Beside herself with rage, she flung the saucepan to the floor. As the eggs smeared over the floor, the boiling water splashed onto Simone's lower legs. She screamed and, in shock and pain, fled from the kitchen. My Li ran and collected his satchel, and then searched the paddocks for Simone.

He had a good inclination where he might find her – at a spot near the creek where he had often seen her sitting. When he caught up with her she was whimpering and trying to prevent her gingham dress from rubbing against her scalded legs. As My Li approached, Simone looked up in terror. For a moment My Li imagined it was Tiao's frightened face he was seeing.

Since leaving Canton, both My Li and Kinqua had picked up and accumulated an understanding of English words and phrases, My Li at a faster rate than Kinqua.

'Don't run!' said My Li. 'Don't be afraid! I can help you...' My Li helped Simone separate her dress from where it had adhered to her skin. He poured a soothing salve over the burns and gave her the jar, explaining in faltering English, with many gesticulations, that she should apply it frequently to keep the wounds moist. Then he left her alone under the tree.

A few days later, as My Li was running past the forge on an errand, the blacksmith grabbed My Li by his arm, thrusting his bearded face close to My Li's until their noses nearly met. 'If I hear of you touching Simone again, you yellow bastard, I'll tear you apart!'

His grip on My Li's arm left a bruise that turned black and then green before fading. From that day on, the Chinese always wanted My Li to be with whoever was detailed to collect their meals or rations, for whenever My Li was present, there would be delicacies like treacle and honey included with the more mundane items.

In the twilight after they had finished their supper, the Chinese would gather and smoke their clay pipes and talk about the day's events and China – home. But My Li, although he was as Chinese as his countrymen and felt the sentimental tug of his country's life-style and traditions, was unable to think of China as home. It was a country which could permit the random and wanton slaying of innocents like Tiao; a country which could accept the ostracism and persecution of people like Song Li – forced by circumstances to lead a different kind of life to that acceptable to others. Such a country was incapable of earning his emotional and patriotic allegiance. My Li felt as if he did not belong anywhere, and often, with increasing frequency, he sought his own company.

As the sun set one evening, illuminating the western horizon with red rays, Kinqua, worried that My Li's absences were becoming a bad habit, went to find him. It did not take Kinqua long. My Li was collecting herbs from the paddocks along the watercourse. Not far away, as if her presence was totally accidental, Simone was nonchalantly wandering towards her favourite nook near the creek.

Kinqua smiled knowingly, pleased to see My Li was not becoming morbidly solitary and estranged from human company. But then his face frowned and he worriedly looked back to where the forge was lit scarlet in the dimming light.

CHAPTER TEN

Even legally indentured Chinese immigrants of the day were compelled, by legislation, to obey all reasonable demands of their employers − for which they were paid five shillings for working an eighty to one hundred-hour week.

Throughout the colonies, there were numerous cases of double-dealing and inhumane treatment being meted out by callous employers. The Chinese had little recourse to the law. The difference in languages was a major cause of discrimination and, even if individual problems were finally heard by the Courts, most magistrates found in favour of the employers with whom they mixed socially and with whom they shared the same colour skin.

Although he had no legal right to forcibly detain the Chinese from the Dayspring, MacArthur turned out to be a fair man who kept his word to those whose labour he had commandeered. So long as the kidnapped Chinese worked when and where required and accepted MacArthur's autocratic authority – and his thugs were always prepared to persuade those among them who did not – they were well treated. They were fed, housed, albeit primitively, and clothed. Each man received a pair of boots, trousers and a shirt over the duration of their detention.

In the eyes of the law, the Chinese were illegal immigrants, and they feared bringing bureaucratic interest upon themselves by drawing attention to their plight.

By common consent they decided to work the year MacArthur required for them, and to make and save as much money as they could to pay the Government Entrance Tax. Once the tax was paid, they would become legal immigrants, free to travel the country and to go about their business. Those who were too spendthrift, enjoyed gambling to excess or were simply too lazy to save for their Entrance Tax, would have to continue working for MacArthur another year. By the end of the year the majority of the Dayspring's Chinese were financially able to pay their own taxes and move on.

Kinqua raised his extra funds by adding some unusual dishes to the MacArthurs' dining-table. Not only did he scour the paddocks for edible fungi, giving the bulk to the cook and keeping the remainder for their own use, Kinqua also rescued and revived the station's sole strawberry plant. It had been planted the previous spring in an attempt to bring sweetness and variety to the MacArthur's diet but had withered and been given up for lost during the following dry summer months when rain did not fall for such a long time, the creek on which their lives depended ceased to flow.

Kinqua noticed that a sucker still showed signs of life and, digging it up, he replanted it closer to the remaining water-holes along the course of the creek, so he did not have to carry the water necessary to nurture it so far. With attentive care in his precious spare time and the aid of a small fence made of wattle sticks to protect the plant from the sheep and other herbivores, the strawberry plant recovered and flourished. Kinqua soon had runners extending in all directions.

When the luscious fruit appeared and ripened, Kinqua endeared himself to the cook by suggesting some succulent deserts that could be created by utilising the available cream, eggs and sugar as ingredients. The deserts brought the cook acclaim from MacArthur's grateful family. They were a delectable treat where monotonous tastes were the norm. The cook was constantly racking his brain for ways to supplement and bring diversity to his employer's meals, and it turned out that Kinqua knew a number of delicious recipes.

The cook paid Kinqua to keep the strawberries and recipes coming. 'Where did you learn these things?' My Li asked Kinqua.

'I was once an advisor to a great Lord, and had to be at his side at all times – including whenever he ate. I had plenty of time to observe the delicacies that graced his table.'

Kinqua's words reminded My Li that he knew nothing of his aged friend's past.

He pointed his realisation out to Kinqua.

Kinqua smiled. 'These days my past outweighs my future – but my interest is in the future and the past must not be permitted to intrude upon the present.'

My Li made his money charging small fees for his herbal remedies.

True to his word, when the Chinese had worked for him for one year, MacArthur collected the Entrance Tax fees from those who could afford it, and made appropriate application on their behalf to the magistrate at Windsor. After the usual administrative delay, receipts were received verifying their taxes had been paid. When the receipts were distributed, the Chinese who held them in their hands were free to leave the MacArthur's sheep-run.

As the end of their year of forced labour approached, and the Chinese who had the money began to make their plans to leave and march to the gold-fields, My Li surreptitiously met with Simone. Simone had a bruised cheek. 'Mother?'

'Father.'

'Why don't you come with us? There is nothing keeping you here.'

The ramifications of the idea took time to register. 'My parents,' Simone thought aloud. 'They might try to stop me.'

'They might not.'

Simone squinted at My Li over her swollen face. 'It might be possible,' she said slowly. 'You are my only friend here – and Kinqua, of course. But that isn't the same, and it won't be the same after you've gone.'

'When we leave, we will have to cross the creek at the ford. If you decide to come with us, wait for us on the far side of the creek. There is a clump of trees and scrub where you could hide until we come past.'

Simone left My Li feeling happier than she had ever felt before.

Ever since My Li had met him, Kinqua had regularly made it his practice to meditate. He usually did so in the evenings, when most of the Chinese were having their discussions about the day's activities.

My Li was returning from his clandestine meeting with Simone when he came across Kinqua, sitting in the middle of the saddle-horses' paddock, his legs folded under him in a lotus position, his face towards the setting sun. Kinqua's eyes were closed. To My Li, he was a picture of serenity. Whereas Kinqua was an esoteric soul, My Li, partly because of the experiences that had blighted his short life, and partly because of the practical nature of his training as an apothecary, saw little value in Kinqua's inactivity.

My Li decided to wait for his friend. As he sat on the ground, Kinqua heard him and turned to determine the reason for the noise.

'I didn't mean to startle you.'

'Then you shouldn't have.'

'I couldn't help it.'

'We are all responsible for our actions.'

'Why do you meditate Kinqua? What do you get out of it?'

'My meditation is the well at which I drink. If a person is on their correct path through life, they have within them motivations like faith and hope. But sometimes life's noisy problems obscure what is good, so sensible people replenish themselves at the well of tranquillity and fortify themselves to meet their next misfortune.'

'Do you really believe that?' My Li's reply was cynical.

'Yes, and so should you. Because what you imagine will be what you become. The mind can move mountains. That is why you should always think positive thoughts. Even if you have to think sad thoughts, think positively about those thoughts that make you sad and you will be uplifted.'

My Li shook his head. 'I would like to believe that but I cannot.'

'The application of heat and steam will straighten crooked wood. All things are possible,'

But My Li was not impressed by what he saw as Kinqua's simplistic outlook. When Kinqua meditated, he meditated without My Li's company.

CHAPTER ELEVEN

The Chinese had been warned that the journey to the diggings would be a dangerous one but they were undeterred. The lure of the precious yellow metal was as strong as the will to live among some of them. Most had been counting the days until they were due to leave in eager anticipation.

'Who knows,' a Chinese excitedly cried. 'I might get lucky and be able to buy Kwantung province when I get home!'

The white workers were contemptuous.

'You've got no idea what you're getting into!' they scoffed. 'There are thousands of square miles of emptiness out there! If you don't get lost, and are never heard of again, you will probably die of thirst – and if you don't die of thirst, you will probably die with an Aborigine's shovel nosed spear between your ribs!'

The Chinese learnt that the track they were to follow to the gold-fields led for hundreds of kilometres through country where no white man willingly went. The Aboriginal tribes in the area were warlike, and a number of would-be miners had been ambushed and speared to death in retaliation for what the Aborigines saw as incursions into their tribal lands. The place where most of the attacks had taken place was a gorge known as Heaven's Gate.

Once through the gorge, it was a relatively safe hike to the gold-fields. It was because many miners did not get through the gorge that it was known as Heaven's Gate.

The weeks before the Chinese left were spent preparing for their march. The year working on the MacArthur's property had taught them what they would require to survive. A small gun that fired pellets to shoot birds or kangaroo was essential; so were the animal bladders they accumulated to carry water; and the packs they made from possum fur and other marsupial skins in which to carry their supplies. By retaining portions of their rations, they were able to build up a stock of flour, dried meat, salt, tea; and a tinder-box to take with them.

Their departure was made without fanfare.

Because of what seemed to be a never-ending series of delays as one after another of the men remembered certain things they had forgotten to pack or details that had to be told to the cook or foreman to ensure the smooth running of the property in their absence, they were later in leaving than they hoped.

'The place will still function without you,' My Li irritably admonished Kinqua, who was among those responsible for their lateness in leaving.

'I can't help it,' replied Kinqua. 'I don't want to be blamed if something goes wrong.'

'But you won't be here!'

'I know. It's stupid isn't it? But I can't help myself.'

The small party of Chinese determined to reach the gold-fields numbered fifteen. They did not get away from the homestead until well after sunrise. The white workers had been going about their duties since before dawn and their farewells were confined to the Chinese destined to remain behind for another year or until such time as they found the funds for their Entrance Tax.

'I'm going to come with you,' one of the men decided at the last minute. My Li and Kinqua knew him as an incorrigible gambler who preferred to throw dice than work. The man had not paid his tax.

'But when we get to the gold-fields, you will have to produce your Entry Tax receipt before the police will issue you with a license to mine or stake a claim. What will you do then?'

Dismayed, the man changed his mind and vowed to change his ways as well.

'Keep looking over your shoulder. I'll be right behind you; you wait and see!'

But My Li knew the man would not change, and would have to work for at least another year before following them to the diggings.

As the party bound for the gold-fields left the huts that had been their homes for so long, the cook came out of the kitchen and pressed enough sandwiches for all of them into Kinqua's arms. Kinqua and the cook had become friendly as a result of their commercial relationship and often enjoyed conversing with each other.

'Goodbye my friend. You take some of the sunshine with you. Good luck and may we meet again!'

There was no sign of Simone as they marched past the sheep yards where Kinqua and My Li had protected the newly weaned lambs from predators long into the night and raked the ground clean of dung in a stench of sheeps' urine that clung to their clothes for days.

When they reached the shallow wagon ford across the creek, My Li and Kinqua dropped back to the rear of the party. As the group splashed across, some leaping from rock to rock to keep their feet dry, My Li and Kinqua fell further behind.

When the other Chinese drew ahead, My Li darted into the trees. 'Simone! Are you there? Are you coming with us?'

My Li dashed between the clumps of scrub. 'Simone! Where are you?'

But Simone was not waiting for them.

Her father was. As My Li drew abreast with the bleached stump of a ring-barked tree, the blacksmith emerged from where he had been hiding. One vicious punch sent a surprised My Li sprawling across the grass.

The blacksmith towered over him. 'So you thought she'd run away with you, did you? You thought my little girl would run off with a bunch of chinks. Well, even Simple Simone has got more sense than to run off with the likes of you. She told me everything, and she told me to give you one from her. Cop that!'

The blacksmith kicked My Li in his ribs. The pain from the blow seared through his lightweight frame and he scrambled to evade the second boot that followed the first.

'Don't!' shouted Kinqua, coming to My Li's aid. 'Stop it! You will kill him.'

If the blacksmith's boots had caught My Li again, the impact of the blow would have undoubtedly caved his ribs and done irreparable damage to his internal organs. But Kinqua threw himself onto the blacksmith's back and hung on tightly.

'Run My Li!'

'Not without you,' gasped My Li, and grabbed hold of the blacksmith's ankles, preventing him from lashing out with his boots. Hearing their yells, the other Chinese, further up the track, returned just as the blacksmith managed to dislodge Kinqua, tossing him like a rider bucked from a horse, into the, thankfully, soft grass. The returning Chinese hurriedly dragged My Li and Kinqua to their feet and formed a protective cordon between the blacksmith and his victims. But the blacksmith felt he had made his point.

'Let that be a lesson to you!' he shouted, shaking his fist as the Chinese retreated back up the track, taking My Li and Kinqua with them.

'It doesn't make sense to me,' Kinqua said to My Li an hour later as they glumly walked away from MacArthur's sheep-run. 'There is something amiss with this.'

My Li shook his head in disagreement. His left eye, which had taken the full impact of the blacksmith's fist, was rapidly closing.

'No there's not. It's simple. She made a fool of me. And if you say anything philosophical, I'll hit you myself.'

'There's more to this than meets the eye,' repeated Kinqua, pointing to My Li's black eye. 'Perhaps you are becoming one-eyed.'

CHAPTER THIRTEEN

Kinqua was correct to doubt My Li's belief he had been duped. Simone had been on her way to the meeting-place near the ford when her father learnt of her intention to leave with My Li and Kinqua.

She had picked her moment well, having waited until the MacArthur family's breakfast was ready and then volunteering to deliver one of the trays to the house herself when a domestic servant was either tardy or delayed in returning to the kitchen to collect it.

Only the domestic servants were allowed inside the homestead and Simone waited at the back door until the flustered servant gratefully accepted the tray from her. Safely out of her mother's sight, Simone ran to her parents' hut to collect the hold-all with a draw-string into which she had packed her meagre possessions. She was almost to the doorway when her father, returning unexpectedly, blocked it.

'What are you doing here?' he demanded, knowing Simone should still be in the kitchen with her mother. Then he saw the bag in her hand and his brow furrowed.

'Where do you think you're going?' His voice was menacing. Simone could not believe her bad luck. Her father rarely returned from the forge before the midday meal once he had gone to work. She did not reply. Her father snatched the hold-all from her hand.

'What's in here then?'

He emptied the contents of the bag on to the packed dirt floor. Simone's favourite dress, her underwear and assorted hairpins and toilet accessories were spilled into the light of day. Her father picked up the framed mirror, the size of her hand, which Simone had been given for Christmas by the MacArthurs when in a benevolent mood.

The blacksmith stared quizzically at his daughter.

'Where do you think you're going? Do you think you're going somewhere do you? Whatever gave you that idea? Well, speak up.'

Simone remained silent. Her father cuffed her. 'Tell me what you were up to or that won't be the only slap you get?'

'I won't tell you,' Simone replied bravely.

'We'll see about that!' snarled her father and, as he lifted his hand to strike her again, her mother appeared, wiping her hands on her grimy apron.

'So this is where you got to. There's a pile of washing up waiting for you my girl! I was wondering what had happened to you [space]...'

Simone's mother saw the bag in her husband's hand and the dress and Simone's belongings on the floor.

'... what's this then?'

'She was leaving us. I caught her.'

'Leaving us? What for? Where were you going girl?'

'I know where she was going. She was going to go off to the gold-fields with that young Chink and the rest of them. That's what she was going to do!'

Simone's mother was horrified. 'Go with the Chinamen! Surely not. You've got to have standards in life girl! Where's your pride? Not Chinamen!'

Simone refused to answer. 'Answer your mother, Simone.'

Simone had nothing to say. Her father clouted her hard across the side of her head. 'Well? What have you got to say for yourself? Is what your father says is true? Speak up Miss Hoity-Toity!'

Simone pressed her lips together.

Her mother folded her flabby arms. 'Hit her husband! The bitch is getting above herself!'

Simone weathered several solid blows before she burst into tears and begged her father to stop. But he was not listening and the punishment he inflicted was cruel. Simone told them everything. She confessed what was intended and where she was to meet My Li.

Consequently, instead of finding Simone waiting for them on the far side of the ford, My Li and Kinqua encountered the blacksmith.

Hours after the party of Chinese resumed their westerly march to the gold-fields and the blacksmith had returned triumphant to his forge, two Chinese tinkers – itinerant salesmen selling and mending pots, kettles and other household utensils – bowed by the weight of the loads on their backs, walked into the MacArthur homestead along the track from the north east. When they stated who they were and what they offered, 'Fix anything! Fix it cheap!' they were directed to the cookhouse.

'We've got our own smithy here,' the cook told them. 'We do all our own fixing.'

According to bush etiquette, it would have been bad manners to send the pair of tinkers on their way without offering them a tin of tea and something to eat. It was also customary to exchange information about the state of the track and news from the outside world.

The Chinese tinkers' knowledge of English was limited but a discussion ensued while the Chinese drank their tea and devoured some left over slices of lamb between slabs of bread baked that day.

'Where we sleep boss?'

'You can bunk down by the woolshed or, if you prefer to keep to yourselves, there's a good spot with clean water near the ford. Which way are you heading?'

The Chinese looked at each other. One shrugged his shoulders and replied, 'It depends.' Then he added, 'any Chinese around here?'

The kindly cook laughed.

'You want to talk in your own lingo, do you? Fair enough. Yes – we've got a few Chinese here. But if you had been here this morning, you would have met a lot more of your kind. You could have had a party. You've missed them though. They have gone to the gold-fields.'

The two tinkers looked at each other again.

'I'll leave you to finish your meal in peace,' the cook said to them. 'Give me a yell when you have finished and I'll give you some more if you are still hungry.'

Unknown to the kindly Cook, Simone had been locked in the cold store by her mother and father to prevent her running after My Li and Kinqua when their backs were turned. Even if the cook had been aware of Simone's predicament, it was highly unlikely he would have aroused her father's fury by letting Simone out. In the cook's domain, Simone's mother did as she was told, but outside of the kitchen, the portly cook was no match for the blacksmith.

'We'll let you out tonight,' Simone's parents had promised her. It will be too late for you to try catching up to them then!'

On hearing the cook conversing with the two Chinese tinkers, battered and sore Simone gingerly climbed onto a packing box and gazed through the tiny window in the wall. It was too small for her to squeeze through and gauze covered to keep out flies, but it allowed air flow and encouraged cool air to circulate inside.

The Chinese were sitting in the shade of the cold store, less than a few metres from the window.

To Simone, most Chinese looked the same, except when familiar with them, as she was now familiar with My Li. It did not occur to her that the Chinese, sitting eating below and along from where she stood at the window, were strangers and did not belong on the sheep-run. Simone took it for granted that any Chinese on the station would know My Li and that message might eventually get to him.

'Tell My Li,' she whispered through cut and broken lips to the Chinese tinker when the cook went back inside the kitchen. 'Tell My Li my parents caught me. If he can get word to me of his whereabouts, I'll try and find him.'

The two tinkers were surprised to see Simone's face at the gauze. But when they heard the name My Li they gave her their undivided attention. Getting to their feet, they said, 'My Li! My Li! Where is My Li?'

They responded as if they knew My Li well, and Simone assumed they were acquaintances.

'Over the ford to the gold-fields. He's on the road to Heaven's Gate. Catch up with him – please! Tell him Simone got caught! Tell him Simone needs help!'

The bigger of the two tinkers grinned evilly. 'Don't worry Missy. We'll find him and tell him. Don't worry.'

'Please hurry.' urged Simone.

'We will,' promised the other tinker. 'We will,' he assured her. And for the first time Simone noticed the taller of the two tinkers had an unsightly livid red scar where his nose joined his upper lip.

The tinkers were the Red Poles sent in pursuit of My Li. After an ocean voyage on a ship with conditions as bad, if not worse than those experienced by My Li and Kinqua; after three months prying and inquiring in boorish Sydney Town taverns trying to discover what had happened to the passengers aboard the Dayspring – the ship that had to bury so many men at sea because of an outbreak of cholera.

After finally getting a clue from a drunken Chinese who had been aboard that awful ship and who now worked for a sheep grazier at Braidwood; after tramping two thirds of, what was to them, the uncivilised tail-end of the world, to properties owned by Wentworth and Blaxland — they had found, in a primitive and desolate region of the colony, that My Li was alive and en route to the gold-fields.

With a death penalty on them if they failed to return to China with the seal of the Triad, the Red Poles felt they had struck rich pay dirt of their own.

CHAPTER THIRTEEN

After wolfing down the remains of the meal given to them by the cook, the Red Poles set out after My Li and the party of Chinese, to the gold-fields.

Having crossed the ford, the Red Poles dumped the pots and pans and the paraphernalia associated with their disguise as tinkers among the trees where the blacksmith had lain in wait for My Li. Retaining only two hessian bag, into which they dropped food and drink to sustain them, they knotted lengths of ropes around the open ends and then fastened the loose ends to the corner, enabling the sacks to be slung across their backs. Then they continued on their way. The release from their heavy burdens gave impetus to their swiftly padding feet, and the knowledge they were only hours away from catching up with the widow Song Li's son and certain of seizing back the seal of the Triad, filled them with euphoric elation. The rules of the Triad did not excuse failure. Unless the Red Poles exacted the Triad's penalty for the theft of the seal and returned with the ring to their masters, they were destined to continue to pursue My Li with all the pitiless implacability of the mythological Greek Eurinys or Furies, who brought vengeance to the house of Agamemnon.

Lack of success on their part would eventually result in ostracism by their brethren and, ultimately, their own lives would be forfeited as the price for their ineffectual pursuit.

Although anxious to bring a quick end to their year-long chase, there was nothing hurried or over-excited about the manner in which the Red Poles alternatively jogged and walked quickly along the track; just unrelenting determination to, at all costs, succeed. Their pace was faster than that set by My Li and Kinqua's party, and the Red Poles should have caught up with them later that night, after the fifteen prospective gold miners stopped to camp and rest. But they did not.

At the same time as the Red Poles were starting out from the MacArthur homestead, My Li, Kinqua and their companions were engaged in an argument. It was nothing to do with what they saw as My Li's stupidity in getting involved with the blacksmith and his daughter. Several of the Chinese had had their own differences with the blacksmith. Some had also suffered from his fists.

Their argument was not a falling out – more a heated discussion.

Having left the vicinity of the sheep-run, the terrain of which they had acquired local knowledge of over the previous year, they were now, for the first time, confronted by open country they were unfamiliar with. One of the Chinese had a crudely drawn map on a cleaned and stretched possum skin indicating the way to the diggings. Carefully put together from snippets of information collected in conversations with MacArthur's white employees and travellers passing through, they compared the features they were looking at with the details indicated on the map.

In front of them rose a series of low mesas; hills eroded flat by wind and water and, a hundred metres from where they stood, the track they were following divided.

One fork led straight on towards the mesas whilst the other went in a long loop around to their left, until it disappeared out of sight behind the shoulder of the farthest mesa. The map showed that the tracks reunited on the far side of the mesas, and both tracks appeared equidistant on the map. The debate was over which track was preferred.

Ah Wei, who was the Chinese in charge of the map, was for taking the most direct route.

'It will be quicker. If we take the track that detours around the hills it could take us many extra hours.'

'But at least we know the other track is level and easy to walk,' said another Chinese, a middle-aged man with a drooping moustache.

'We can see it from here. We don't know what the other track through the mesas is like. We can't see it.'

'I would rather take the track around the mesas that we can see,' offered Kinqua.

'So would I,' said My Li, thinking of Kinqua's aging muscles. 'What are a few more hours on the road if the way is easy?'

The four older of the fifteen Chinese agreed with him. The others were younger and impatient.

'It is now well over a year since we left China for the goldfields. I want to find my fortune and leave this barbaric country to the white men as soon as I can.'

The speaker was a man in his early twenties and the other young men concurred with him.

'The track through the middle will be the quickest,' they echoed adamantly.

Rather than split the party, the elder men acquiesced and tramped after the younger men as they led the way towards the mesas, standing out starkly in the afternoon light.

Other than the sound of their shuffling feet and the crunch of gravel underfoot, there was little other noise.

Both Kinqua and My Li wore straw hats they had woven to protect themselves from the bite of the sun. My Li's was a traditional cone-shaped coolies' hat and Kinqua's was wide-brimmed like a flat sombrero. Some of the other Chinese also wore hats. There were two cabbage-tree hats of the kind white men wore but most of them, mainly the younger men, were bareheaded.

Ah Wei, who carried the map, also carried a parasol made from possum skins to shade himself from the harsh sun.

Sometimes, when the track was wide enough, two or three men walked side by side in subdued conversation but mostly, as the heat sapped body fluids and caused spirits to become enervated, they walked without speaking.

It was the silence and emptiness of the country that was so alien and daunting to the Chinese. The thuds of kangaroo breaking cover at their approach still caused consternation and made them skittish and fearful of Aboriginal attack. The sudden cries of the birds they disturbed were always alarming in the weighty silence, continually shocking them from their mindless, though mobile, lethargy.

The cloudless, blue domed sky that stretched from horizon to horizon; the sepulchral vastness and the dirge of cicadas as the afternoon advanced, combined to give My Li the impression that he was walking to the end of the earth and that, at some point they would come to the edge of the land mass, where, careful they did not fall off the edge, they could gaze into Eternity.

The further the track took them among the mesas, the more its surface worsened. At times it disappeared entirely, washed away by a downpour distant in time and they had to scour around before finding it again as it twisted and turned through the mesas. Sometimes they found it difficult to tell the difference between the track and the walkways used by wallabies and runaway sheep.

Once they thought they were on the track but then realised they were lurching down a gully that led them nowhere. They had to turn and retrace their steps.

As the hours passed, the younger men who had vehemently insisted they take the direct route became subdued. They appreciated that they would have already cleared the mesas and be marching with them at their backs had they taken the easier route recommended by their elders.

As night fell, they were still kilometres short of the plain on the far side, and all had cuts and abrasions where they had slipped and fallen on the loose stony scree at the base of the mesas. They wearily decided to make camp among the last of the mesas and continue across the plain in the morning. Ah Wei found a small pool of water among the rocks, but as he was lowering himself to drink, he slipped and, to stop himself falling, snatched at a spiky bush for support. Ah Wei was the last to fall asleep, having spent hours painfully extracting thorns from his hand.

When the Red Poles reached the fork, they had no doubt which direction to take. Without slackening their stride they tool the obviously easier track to the left. While My Li and Kinqua were scrambling along the difficult route through the mesas, the Red Poles had already gone around them and were crossing the open plain in hot pursuit of My Li and his disgruntled comrades, who, unknown to the Red Poles, had been left far to their rear.

CHAPTER FOURTEEN

The Red Poles slept without a fire on the open plain, breaking camp at first light. It took them only three or four minutes to pack up. They stood up, brushed the grass seed from their clothes, took a swig from their water bags and started walking.

As the sun rose and warmed their backs, they saw a distant range of undulating hills on the skyline far ahead. It became apparent to the Red Poles that the mesas behind them were geological forerunners to what was yet to come. As they steadily decreased the gap between themselves and the far away hills, already hazy in the morning heat, the bulges grew higher and became more rugged in appearance.

Amazed they had not caught up to My Li and his companions, they pushed themselves harder, sweating profusely as they felt the full force of the sun. But they did not reach the foothills of the range until noon the following day. By then they could see clefts and gaps in the vegetation where rock-falls had torn away topsoil and trees, exposing the bare sedimentary strata in great wound-like swathes across the cliffs.

In the early afternoon the Red Poles began to climb, and the track joined another from the north east, obviously more frequently used than the path they had followed from the mesas. Rusted metal utensils and frayed bits and pieces of clothing occasionally littered the track; thrown aside by miners lightening their loads.

The grassland over which they had been travelling gave way to sparsely treed boulder strewn slopes.

The hills and scarps to either side began to creep nearer and nearer until they towered over the Red Poles as they panted up the track. The track started to twist and wind; at times narrowing and wedging the Red Poles between sheer rock to one side and a precipitous and undoubtedly fatal drop to the other.

Any slip would result in a fall of hundreds of metres, as the track was now half-way up a rock face and compliantly following the bends and turns in the wall. Their hitherto rapid pace slowed to a crawl as they carefully picked their way, one following the other, along the tortuously dangerous path.

As the afternoon wore on, the track began to slope downwards and the Red Poles saw that the cliff they were warily negotiating had brought them into proximity with another vertical wall; parallel but varying between two to three hundred metres apart. Gradually the track they were travelling declined until they reached the floor of what was a gorge. A valley hemmed in by the two perpendicular cliffs. Although the Red Poles did not know its name, they were passing through Heaven's Gate, the gorge the Chinese with Kinqua and My Li had been warned about: the place renowned for ambushes and attacks by marauding Aboriginals on miners going to the gold fields.

The bottom of the gorge was rich with native shrubs and the bird life they attracted was prolific. It was like a hidden green oasis in the midst of the parched brown plains that surrounded the mountain range it provided a pass through. Water oozed through the porous rocks from above, encouraging growth and regeneration. Though unaware of the history of the place, the Red Poles felt a presence other than themselves.

A single white cockatoo shrieked raucously and flew away at their approach. The Red Poles stopped in mid-stride. Unlike Europeans, the Chinese associated white – not black – with funerals and the dead. The cockatoo's flapping wings and cries were piercingly loud and reverberated off the walls of the gorge. The sight had a supernatural fascination to the younger Red Pole. It reminded him of a lonely soul departing for the hereafter.

Night falls quickly in the outback and the Red Poles had not cleared the gorge by the time it grew dark; earlier than usual because the gorge's high walls blocked out the setting sun's rays. They bivouacked by a small pool of water that had collected among the scree at the base of one of the cliff faces. Not having eaten properly for forty-eight hours – they had persisted with short breaks and eaten only dried foods in their attempt to catch up with My Li and his party – the Red Poles lit a camp-fire to cook some rice and recuperate from their self-imposed deprivation.

When their meal was finished, Chang, the Red Pole with the mutilated nose, produced a bottle of rice whiskey from the sack of supplies he carried. The Red Poles had taken a mouthful each and were quietly discussing whether or not it was possible they might have somehow missed the party they were pursuing when Chang noticed a shadow, cast by the flickering fire, move from beside one large rock to behind another. Chang kept talking; consciously preventing any urgency to invade his voice and give away, to whoever or whatever was hiding among the rocks, that they or it had been observed.

At the same time Chang indicated the direction of their danger with repeated stabs of his forefinger. His associate, Yung, understood immediately, and they mentally prepared themselves to cope with whatever was about to happen. Both Red Poles slowly retreated from the light of the flames.

Skilled in dozens of ways to kill with their hands, the Red Poles had no weapons other than their razor sharp reflexes and the knives in their belts. As their sense of impending peril and vulnerability grew, their conversation diminished until it stopped all together. The Red poles strained their ears and eyes for clues to what was going on. Then, what Chang had assumed was another shadow, noiselessly guided forward into the firelight and stood motionless in front of them.

It was a man: a tall, lean Aborigine. The black skin of his flattened nose had a wavy white line painted across it. Other totemic symbols patterned his body.

Tribal markings in the form of raised cicatrice welts stood out boldly on his chest and his curly hair was tied in a bun on top of his head.

His clothing was scant; a penis pouch and a piece of cloth tied as a sweat-band around his forehead.

In his right hand, held non-threateningly upright, were a long spear and a nulla-nulla or throwing-stick, an Aboriginal invention that gave extra leverage to the range and velocity of a thrown spear. Over one shoulder was a dilly-bag of woven grass in which he carried food and his fire sticks.

As if responding to a signal, other Aboriginals moved forward into the light of the fire. The Red Poles' sixth sense, rather than sound or movement, told them there were Aboriginals behind them as well.

Yung smiled warmly and broadly to the warriors. Welcoming them in Chinese, Yung gestured to the Aborigines to gather around the fire and sit down.

For an interminable minute the Aborigines did not move or speak. Neither Chang or his fellow Red Pole could tell if their intentions were hostile or not. Copying Yung, Chang patted the ground beside him, encouraging the Aborigines to join them beside the fire.

Finally, the first Aboriginal spoke rapidly in his own tongue to another Aboriginal standing somewhere behind the two Red Poles. He was answered and, with the clicking of wooden spear shafts against throwing-sticks and boomerangs, the Aboriginals crowded into the fire's circle where, by force of numbers, they took over the Red Pole's encampment. The Red Poles sat helplessly as one of the Aboriginals took it upon himself to investigate the contents of their food sacks.

Another Aboriginal poked Chang with the butt of his spear and said something to his companion who burst out laughing. Chang assumed whatever had been said to be derogatory. Only then did he notice his colleague was still holding the bottle of rice whiskey.

'Would you like a drink?' Chang asked the Aboriginals. 'Drink!' he repeated, mimicking to drink from an imaginary bottle. 'Would you like some?'

The Aboriginals only reaction was to stare dubiously at Chang's pantomime performance.

'Give me the bottle,' Chang demanded. Yung passed over the bottle. 'Ask them if they would like to drink! Do what I did!'

Yung took up the refrain.

'Drink? Do you want a drink?'

He too tilted a make-believe bottle and, lowering it, smacked his lips in satisfaction before wiping his mouth with the back of his hand.

While the Aboriginals' attention was centred on watching Yung's pantomime, Chang took a tiny vial from his pocket and, keeping it hidden within his hand, he poured the contents of the vial into the bottle. Dropping the empty vial into his lap, and placing his thumb over the open neck of the bottle, Chang lifted the bottle and pretended to drink. The rice whiskey and whatever was in the vial instantly mingled.

The Aboriginals had got the gist of Yung's performance and the warrior who had initially appeared reached for the bottle. The Aboriginal lifted it to his lips.

He sipped once, suspiciously, at the contents, frowned, and had the bottle snatched from his hand by another Aboriginal who took a mouthful, spluttered and swallowed and passed the bottle to the man next to him, who did likewise. Chang superciliously grinned at his own success.

The Red Poles remained seated on the ground, beaming at the Aborigines and nodding their approval as the Aboriginals took turns to drink, one after the other, until the contents of the bottle were gone.

CHAPTER FIFTEEN

Following in the footsteps of the Red Poles, it took My Li and Kinqua's party of Chinese, travelling at a pace suited to the eldest and slowest, three days to reach Heaven's Gate. There was little talk as they wound round the hazardous approaches to the gorge. They all knew its reputation. Besides, they were preoccupied with ensuring they did not trip over the man in front's heels and pitch head first down the cliff.

My Li was the exception.

'Did I tell you what they told me back at MacArthur's?'

'No,' said Kinqua, his eyes stuck to the track. 'Is it relevant?'

'I hope not! One of the white station-hands said the Aboriginals prefer the flesh of yellow men to whites.'

'Why is that?' responded Kinqua.

'Because we Chinese are sweeter and our flesh lasts longer in the heat.'

'But the Aborigines aren't cannibals are they?'

'Let's hope we don't get the opportunity to find out!'

'It sounds to me like your station-hand was speaking from experience. I think we might have more to fear from the likes of him than the Aborigines.'

Birds of prey circled over the gorge as they entered. My Li and Kinqua had never seen anything like it before. There were at least a hundred kites, hawks and even a Wedge-Tailed Eagle or two soaring one above the other in a vortex-like formation of birds.

Ah Wei, who was leading the Chinese into the gorge, held up his hand and pointed at the birds for the benefit of those who had not noticed them.

'There's something dead ahead of us,' said Kinqua. 'Something large, I suspect.'

Cautiously they moved on.

A few hours later they arrived at the campsite recently vacated by the Red Poles.

Ah Wei recoiled in horror from the sight that met his eyes and called My Li forward. Kinqua went with him. By the pool where the Red Poles had camped were the bodies of a dozen Aboriginals, frozen by rigour mortis in contortions of agony. Some of the corpses had been disturbed by carrion birds and foraging animals. Most of the corpses had their eyes pecked out. The air was loud with the hum of flies and the flapping of wings.

My Li and Kinqua moved among the dead Aboriginals.

An empty bottle lay discarded on the ground. My Li picked it up. Holding the bottle away from his nose he sniffed at the open neck.

'Aniseed,' said My Li. 'I can smell aniseed. There was arsenic in this bottle!'

My Li hurled the bottle into the rocks where it shattered on impact, the fragments tinkling as they settled.

'So they were poisoned.'

'It appears so to me, Kinqua.'

One of the corpses groaned. The frightened Chinese drew back. My Li went to the huddled shape. The Aboriginal's back bore scars where he had accidently rolled into his camp-fire while trying to keep warm during the winter nights, when the temperature could drop from one hundred degrees Fahrenheit in the day to below freezing after dark.

'He is still alive. Perhaps he didn't drink enough to kill him,' said Kinqua.

'Perhaps he was stronger than the rest and the poison is taking longer to finish its work,' replied My Li. The other Chinese stared fearfully about in superstitious terror, thinking of all the agitated spirits that might still be present.

My Li massaged the Aboriginal's stomach, his hands working and manipulating the man's abdominal muscles. The Aboriginal suddenly moaned and retched. My Li repeated the process until his patient had nothing left to bring up. 'This one might recover. We will make a litter and take him with us in the morning.'

'In the morning?'

'To move him now might kill him.'

'And we should bury and give funerals to his friends before continuing,' counselled Ah Wei.

The other Chinese vigorously nodded their agreement, their eyes still wide and fearful. But they were happy to help put the murdered Aboriginals' souls to rest, especially if they were still going to be in the vicinity that night.

'These people don't bury their dead,' Kinqua reminded them. 'They put them up on platforms in trees until their bones are picked clean by scavengers. Then they return to collect the bones and take them for interment somewhere in the land of their birth.'

'How do you know all this?'

'I take an interest in the customs of different peoples. By learning about other people, you discover things about yourself. But if you really want to know, the cook told me.'

'So that's what you two talked about all the time!'

'Not all the time. We talked about lots of topics.'

'Well,' said Ah Wei, 'I'll be happy to put the bodies of these poor people in the trees. The ground is too hard and rocky to dig anyway.'

The Chinese built platforms in the trees by lashing four sturdy poles into rectangular shapes with vines and then lying branches strong enough to bear the weight of a body across them. The most difficult part was lifting the corpses up onto the platforms.

Few had been lying straight when death took them and their twisted limbs made the bodies awkward to handle. Once on the platforms, the Chinese stripped gum trees of their bark and covered the corpses, placing rocks to hold the bark in place like on the roofs of the white settler's huts.

Later that night, the Aboriginal called, 'Ngama! Ngama!' and then asked for water in English.

The Chinese gave the Aborigine water and huddled around the survivor of the massacre. When the Aboriginal first became aware of the affable, smiling, oriental faces looking down at him, he stared back at them in shock.

'Don't be frightened,' the Chinese told him in English and Cantonese. 'We are trying to help you.'

When he had recovered enough to speak, the Chinese discovered they could communicate with him in the language that was foreign to all of them – English. Both the Aboriginal and the Chinese had to struggle to make themselves comprehensible to each other, but as Kinqua said, 'The differences between us are only skin deep.'

By persevering, they made themselves understood. The substance of their conversation went something like this, 'Who did this to you and your friends?'

'Two of your kind. And now you tend to me and let me share your fire. I don't understand.'

'Black man, white man, yellow man,' said Kinqua. 'It makes no difference. Men are only good and bad and indifferent. Where did you learn to speak English.'

'I helped the white men string the talking wire from pole to pole where I live. I showed them where to find water.'

'Where do you live?'

'My country is many walks from here.'

'Then this land is not your land.'

'No.'

'So this land does not belong to you?'

'No. The land belongs to no-one. The land belongs to the Earth Spirit.'

'What were you and your friends doing here if this is not your country?'

'The young men who were with me were the best young warriors of my tribe. I was leading them through the countries of our rivals, a procession to prove our strength and to challenge the best of their men to oppose us. Whoever returns to his own country and the fires of his father after such a sortie is shown respect as a great warrior.'

'How far were you going,' asked Kinqua, hoping to obtain an insight into the land they must travel over to reach the gold-fields.

'To the sacred place.'

'Sacred place? Where is your sacred place?'

'I cannot tell you. Instead, I shall say to him who saved my life – it is where the thorny devils guard the red rock that holds the sky above the earth.'

'Where the thorny devils...? That's certainly a strange answer,' said My Li.

'Cryptic,' added Kinqua.

'So, what happened here?' asked Ah Wei.

'Two of your kind were camped here. They offered friendship and invited us to share their fire and drink. But their bottle contained death.'

'We are going to the white men's gold-fields. We will take you with us. We will carry you until you are well.'

'To where the white men dig the yellow metal?'

'Yes.'

'Then I am content. For a time your path is my path. For I am sure that is where the men who did this foul deed have gone, and I must follow them and slay them so that my tribesmen's spirits might rest. Until they are dead, I am dead. When they are dead, I will then live, and again find the fire of my father.'

A wind rustled the leaves of the trees bearing the bodies of the dead tribesmen, and, for a moment, My Li imagined the murdered tribesmen were acknowledging the Aboriginal's decision.

'And you – who are you? What do we call you?'

'My name is Baracoona. I am the keeper of the Sacred Place.'

'What did the men who gave you the poison look like? Was there anything about them you remember?'

Baracoona thought carefully. 'Yes,' he said. 'One of them had a scar like this,' and he indicated to the welts on his chest, 'here underneath his nose.' And Baracoona pointed to his upper lip.

My Li and Kinqua exchanged glances. 'No', though My Li said to Kinqua, 'there cannot be any connection. It couldn't be the same man. Not the Red Pole. Not there in the Great South Land.'

In the morning, the Chinese made a stretcher from saplings and spare clothes, drawing the sleeves and trouser legs over the poles and buttoning the shirts and flies. They carried Baracoona for four days. At his request, the roughly made stretcher led their march.

The younger Chinese took turns at the poles and were happy to do so – an Aboriginal in their midst, they hoped, might protect them from Aboriginals with aggressive intentions.

On the fifth day Baracoona felt strong enough to walk.

From the stretcher, and when on his own two feet, Baracoona's eyes rarely left the ground. He was following the Red Pole's progress, and learning more about them than they could ever have imagined. 'See there! The one with the scarred nose stopped to urinate there!'

'How do you know it was the one with the scarred nose?'

'He walks on the outside of his right foot. See how the indentation of his footprint is deeper to the outside… It is the same as the footprint where he sat by the camp-fire.'

Baracoona was able to give My Li and Kinqua an approximation of their height, their weight and even whether or not they were tired from the changes in the length of their strides. From examining their faeces, he knew what they were eating.

If Baracoona had been well, he would have been capable of overtaking the Red Poles; possibly of taking his revenge while they slept. But he still suffered from the effects of the poison, and he was forced to remain with the Chinese.

Most of the time Baracoona walked with My Li or Kinqua. On one occasion My Li was so busy trying to get the point of what he was attempting to express to Baracoona across to him, he failed to notice Kinqua had dropped back to the rear of the column. By the time My Li wondered where Kinqua was, the old man had fallen hundreds of metres behind. My Li waited for Kinqua while the rest of their party continued.

'Is something wrong, Kinqua?'

'Just weariness.'

'You are so young in mind that sometimes I forget you are elderly.'

'Who is elderly? When I was twenty, I thought forty was old. At forty I thought fifty over hill. At fifty, sixty did not seem so old. Now…'

My Li affectionately put his arm around the old man. Kinqua was about to say something but as he opened his mouth to speak, My Li said, 'Walk on!' And they both laughed in unison.

Ten days after leaving Heaven's Gate, the trail they were following connected with another. It had been scuffed by lots of feet and had deep ruts dug into it where laden wagons and bullock drays had passed over it. Baracoona stared at where the wheel ruts had sunk into the ground and where the animals' hooves had obliterated the Red Poles' footprints.

'From here you enter the white man's world. The diggings are only a few days ahead. Here I will leave you. Their world is not mine.'

That night they made their farewells.

'Whenever you wish to come, you will be welcome at the fire of my father.'

'What will you do now?' asked Kinqua.

'The ones who killed my brothers are with the whites and they do not like your kind or mine. My place is not there. One day they will leave and when they do, I will know, for I know everything I need to know about them. Let us say goodbye now. When you wake in the morning I will already be gone.'

Ah Wei and the others wished Baracoona well and went to get their sleep. Kinqua and then My Li embraced Baracoona.

'Goodbye Baracoona.'

As My Li and Kinqua went to turn their backs, Baracoona said, 'Wait! Take this with you.'

Delving into his dilly-bag, Baracoona drew out a round piece of wood, no larger than his palm and burnished smooth with handling.

'This is my tjurunga.'

The tjurunga was inscribed with tribal markings.

'If you should need to find me, those of my tribe will know from this you are friends and give you safe passage. Keep it.'

Baracoona pressed the tjurunga into My Li's hands. My Li accepted the tjurunga and, feeling the warmth of the moment, was spurred to give Baracoona something in return, in accordance with his tribal custom.

Kinqua had already turned away in respect for Baracoona and My Li's privacy.

My Li reached under his shirt and from the pocket of his money-belt, still used to conceal the small amount of money they had with them, he drew out the ring that was the seal of the Triad.

'Here! Take this from us.'

My Li went to slip it on Baracoona's finger but the ring was too large. Baracoona felt inside his dilly-bag and drew out a length of hand-rolled twine. Threading the twine through the ring he looped it around his neck and tied the loose ends into a knot. The ring hung against the tribal markings on his chest.

'Where is your land, Baracoona?' asked My Li.

Baracoona lifted his sinewy right arm and, languidly extending it, pointed his forefinger to the north of the descending sun. 'There! There is my country! Many days walk from here. My country is there!' And Baracoona smiled at the thought of his homeland.

When My Li and the others woke the next day, Baracoona had already left them.

CHAPTER SIXTEEN

The Red Poles arrived at the diggings days before My Li, Kinqua, Ah Wei, Baracoona and the others had reached the main road on the outskirts. They attracted little attention as they made their way through the outlying claims. The miners saw them only as two more fortune-hunters – but the Europeans who saw them noted they were two more Chinese, not white men.

There was growing racial discord between Europeans and Chinese on the gold-fields.

At first the white Australians, all migrants themselves, saw no reason to limit the influx of Chinese into the colonies. Some even hoped the Chinese would provide an inexhaustible source of cheap labour. With the end of the transportation of felons from Britain and the transition of the penal settlements into free societies, how else, it was argued, could the squatters replace the convict work-force and develop the country? The answer was, according to the squatters, the use of coloured labour.

In a land where their customs were alien, the Chinese tended to form enclaves for companionship – and mutual protection. As the white miners learnt that nuggets were not waiting for whoever was prepared to bend their knees, as the press had led them to believe, that they were going to have to work back-breakingly hard for their gold, and that the gold was not easy to find, the Chinese were seen as scapegoats by many disillusioned miners.

This problem alone might possibly have been overcome, but, at the time of the mass inflows of Chinese migrant labour into the Australian colonies, the movement towards Workers' Associations was reaching its zenith.

Nowhere was the movement towards unionism stronger than among the mining fraternity. This antagonism was aggravated by short sighted capitalists of the era who used the Chinese, and their willingness to work wherever work was available at rates of pay less than the whites were prepared to accept, as strike-breakers.

As a result, the Chinese became the focus of the white workers' enmity and anger – which grew in ferocity until hatred became entrenched. The economic fears the Europeans originally held for their jobs and futures were modified into pointless, racist persecution of the Chinese simply because their skins were a different pigmentation.

The region where the diggings were located benefited from higher annual rainfall than the country from which My Li's party had come. In fact, the initial find had been because a deluge caused a large washaway in a gully and exposed some nuggets. The main method used to extract the gold bearing ore was alluvial – either by pan or sluicing.

Everywhere the Red Poles looked they could see mounds of debris and men at work. The claims were limited to five hundred and seventy six square feet. If the claim was beside a watercourse, the miners simply shovelled the gravel and sand into pans and swilled the contents with water until only the heaviest particles remained. A glint of gold at the bottom could mean riches and a sudden switch to a luxurious life-style for an, until then, impoverished miner.

Some miners worked their claims as teams. Using water pumped from creeks and dams, and cradles wastefully constructed from rare red cedar – a timber providing long straight boards perfect for the sluice races that were often many metres in length – the miners dug out entire stretches of river banks and beds. The gold was washed from the tons of pebbles and sandy slush by shovelling it into the cradles and sluicing water after it at a fixed volume and rate.

The gold sank to the bottom of the chutes and the miners shared any profits. The miners whose claims were further back from sources of water dug timber-lined shafts deep into the earth in search of subterranean veins of gold. The mines often filled with ground water and even caved in, collapsing on top of their workers. Once in a while, miners found a mother-lode or struck a spot where prehistoric river beds met, ten, twenty or thirty metres down. Places where streams met were popular claims as the junctions caused the water flow to slow and for the heavier gold particles to be deposited. More often, the shafts were sunk at great expense and exertion only to be found unproductive. But the dream of being rich drew miners from all over the world and the unlucky failures were soon replaced by newcomers.

Towns near the gold-fields thrived and grew as they serviced their burgeoning populations. If there was no town near a newly discovered gold-field, a boom town sprang up almost overnight.

Following a motley array of drays, gigs, pony-carts, sulkies and men leading overloaded and swayed-back pack horses, the numbers of which became more numerous as they approached the town, the Red Poles relaxed and slowed their rate of march. Although immensely tired, there was a spring in their walk as they passed between the new clapboard and slab constructed buildings being erected with frantic hammering, sawing and shouting. The widow's son was certain to be close at hand.

121

Their search was nearly over and soon they would be able to return to China to receive the grateful thanks and accolades of their brethren.

But firstly they had to make contact with the local branch of their Triad Society, for even here, in the Great South Land, the ways of the Tongs were practised and rules upheld just as they were in their homeland.

Most of the miners lived in humpies and tents on their claims. Towards the centre of town there were more solid structures, some of stone, like the Christian churches and the Masonic lodge; but the majority, including most of the cottages, the hotels, the newspaper office — the window of which declared it the Clarion, in both English and Chinese — the barber shops, greengrocers, hardware stores, the saddlers and the other shops, were flimsily jerry-built due to their hasty erection to meet the town's extraordinary rapid growth and demand for services. Many of the commercial premises advertised their owner's names. The majority of the names were in Chinese.

At the far end of the main thoroughfare stood an imposing and ornately decorated Chinese temple or joss-house, as the Europeans called it — after the sweet smell of the incense covered joss-sticks being burnt inside.

The Red Poles strode to the joss-house and, recalling their memorised instructions, looked around them and took their bearings. Huddled about the joss-house was the Chinese quarter of the town. Around the Red Poles were restaurants specialising in Chinese cuisine, a shop selling Chinese literature and art, an acupuncturist and a herbalist's shop. There were buildings proclaiming they were fan-tan salons. Although there were no signs advertising their business, the Red Poles knew there were also opium dens close at hand, supplied and run by Triads.

The Red Poles had been given three possible rendezvous. Rendezvous number one was a tea-shop. The Red Poles entered and, after seating themselves at a table near the door, ordered tea. The tea was brought to them on a tray. When the waiter came to collect their empty cups, Chang carefully arranged the cups and tea-pot on the tray. The waiter ignored the Triad recognition sign and merely left them the bill.

An hour or so later, precisely on the hour, they returned to the entrance to the joss-house. A young Chinese miner, his slippers covered in clay, was also waiting near the door. Yung unobtrusively walked over to the miner and said to him softly: 'Are you blind?'

The young miner looked at him blankly and then said, 'of course I'm not. I can see you're mad!' and stalked away.

The weary Red Poles played their final card.

They went to one of the fan-tan salons and sat on a bench on the verandah over-looking the street.

An elderly Chinese was sitting on another bench on the far side of the door. For a time the Red Poles simply sat. Then Chang opened his hessian sack and took out a small tin. Opening the tin, he took out a thin cheroot. Ensuring the elderly Chinese was watching him, Chang lit the cheroot, holding it between the first and second fingers of his left hand, with the end he intended to light towards his chest. After lighting it with a match proffered by the other Red Pole, he flicked the match into the street.

The elderly Chinese saw nothing unusual about the manner in which Chang had lit the cheroot, but a man playing dice at a table inside, had seen him through the window. He got up from the table and moments later stood beside the Red Poles.

'Just arrived?'

The Red Poles nodded.

'The road is hard, how did you walk upon it?'

The Red Poles stiffened with excitement.

'We wore iron soles to our shoes,' replied Chang.

The dice player smiled slyly. 'Before departing, the Five Ancestors composed a verse, which no brethren ever disclosed.'

To which Yung added, 'But if to a brother it is shown he knows at once he is not alone.'

'Follow me please,' said the dice player, and the Red Poles rose and followed the man inside the salon.

The dice player led the Red Poles through the saloon and out its back-door. Without turning to check they were still behind him, the dice player strolled down some back streets with rubbish piled waiting for collection until he came to a nondescript door to an unpainted clapboard building.

He knocked once, then twice quickly and once again. They waited.

There was no response, so the dice player repeated his coded knock. This time the panel in the upper part of the door was swung open and a white face peered at the dice player. Seemingly satisfied with what it saw, the door was opened to admit them.

The face belonged to a scrawny white woman dressed in European garb and wearing an excessive amount of cheap jewellery. It was an attractive face but expressionless. Her eyes were glazed and stared somewhere over the Red Poles' shoulders.

They entered and she shut and bolted the door behind them. The dice player ushered them along a corridor to a door. The woman followed behind.

A male Chinese dressed in western style clothing stood guard on the door.

The dice player made a sign with his fingers and the guard stood aside to allow them to enter. The room was large and had a stage at one end like a meeting-room or hall. It was thrumming with quiet talk and filled with cigar and pipe smoke. At least forty to fifty people were present. Most of them were Chinese but some were European, including two of the half dozen women. They were drinking, playing cards, dice or dominoes. Money and gold dust were freely changing hands.

He motioned to the Red Poles to follow him and, weaving between the tables and the people seated at them, passed through another door on the far side of the room. Closing the door behind them, the Red Poles found themselves in yet another corridor. A corridor lined with four doorways to either side opening off it. From under the closed doors came the sweet, perfumed smell of opium.

At the far end of the corridor was yet another door.

The dice player gave the same knock as he had originally given on the external door. The door opened slightly and the dice player whispered something inaudible to the Red Poles. Then the door was flung open. The guardian was another woman, this time Chinese and wearing a traditional gown, as was a second woman, reclining against cushions on a raised floor to one side of the room. But, unlike the woman who let them in, the second woman was European.

The cushions she was leaning on were huge and colourfully embroidered. The walls behind her were covered in tapestries and the ceiling to the room, much smaller than the hall they had passed through, was decorated with swags of gracefully draped silk. A brazier no bigger than a desert bowl had incense burning in it.

The Red Poles smiled at each other.

After all they had gone through, walking into the room was reminiscent of being back in China. But their pleasure was fleeting. Their attention was drawn to the man seated at the desk opposite the European woman. He too was Chinese. He was leafing through the pages of a ledger of accounts and simultaneously working an abacus at breakneck speed.

The man working the abacus looked up as the dice player approached the desk and kowtowed. The woman who had admitted the Red Poles joined her European companion among the cushions.

'It isn't good enough!' snapped the man with the abacus. 'We are five hundred pounds down this month!'

The dice player responded from his knees on the floor.

'It is the white miners fault Master. Their hate for us knows no bounds. They blame us for everything – including their bad luck and still they refuse to work hard. And now – although we offer them the best deals, the best alcohol, the cleanest women – they are refusing to come as often as they used to. They begrudge our commercial success.'

The man with the abacus tutted.

'It is getting bad. It is going to erupt into violence. I know. I can feel it. We had better send out debt collectors and crack down on all outstanding amounts owing while we can!'

'Yes Master.'

'And this time there will be no extensions of credit for anyone.'

'Yes Master.'

'They pay or else! Do you understand?'

'Yes Master.'

'Good,' purred the man with the abacus, and he shifted his steely gaze to the Red Poles. 'So! You got here at last. Your quarry has taken you on quite a wild-goose chase, hasn't he.'

The Red Poles did not reply.

The man placed his abacus on the desk and, closing the ledger with a thump, stood up from his chair.

The Red Poles could hardly believe their eyes. The man scarcely rose in height. As he came around the desk to stand before them, they understood why. The man was a dwarf.

The dwarf appraised the Red Poles. 'I think they fit the White Fan's description of them, don't you?'

'Yes. Indeed I do Master,' agreed the dice player.

'Welcome brothers,' said the dwarf to the Red Poles. 'Will you kindly show me a sign before we get down to business?'

The Red Poles complied and drew black scarves from their pockets. The dwarf reciprocated. The jaded Red Poles smiled wanly in relief.

'Please be seated,' invited the dwarf. The two women rose quickly and brought cushions for the Red Poles to sit on. The Chinese women then left the room. Still wary, the Red Poles lowered themselves onto the cushions. 'What do I call you?' The dwarf asked the Red Poles.

You may call me Chang. My friend is known as Yung.'

'For your information,' the dwarf said briskly, 'some months ago now, all Black Scarf lodges received a message from our Mistress, yours and mine, instructing us to give you all possible assistance. The word of your coming and its purpose had been spread among the other lodges in this land. We are aware of the importance of your mission. The theft of the seal is a great sin against our Society and for the perpetrator to go unpunished will encourage others to test our strength. Our Mistress informs us that the Society's credibility is at stake. We have pledged the utmost support our lodge can muster, and more … you have only to ask and it will be yours. As you are aware from our prompt contact with yourselves, all roads are being watched.

The Chinese woman returned with a pan of lemon scented warm water and towels, which she placed beside the Red Poles.

'Has he been seen?' asked Yung.

'Not yet,' answered the dwarf. 'We do not believe he has arrived here yet.'

The Red Poles exchanged looks of consternation. 'But that is impossible. The youth and a party of fifteen were no more than a few hours in front of us when we set out to come here.'

'I assure you, no party of Chinese has arrived here in the last week.' Seeing the Red Poles despondency, the dwarf added, 'Don't fret, my executioners. Rest and refresh yourselves. Our facilities are yours. He will be found. He won't escape your tender embrace!'

CHAPTER SEVENTEEN

Stopping well outside the town, My Li, Kinqua, Ah Wei and their party shook hands and embraced. Some wanted to head across country to where they knew their relatives' or friends' claims were located. Some wanted to taste the delights of civilisation again, and continue on into town. The remainder wanted to search for worthwhile claims before going into town to register their finds at the Government Office. After saying their goodbyes, they departed in different directions, leaving My Li, Kinqua and Ah Wei together by the side of the road.

'What do you intend to do?' asked Ah Wei.

My Li shrugged his shoulders.

'My brother Lun-Tan has a claim beside the river to the south,' Ah Wei said, 'It is a good claim and he needs help he can trust. I wrote to him from MacArthur's and received a reply shortly before we set out. His partner decided to sell his share in the claim to my brother, and to leave for China with what gold was his. He would welcome you. My brother is not so young and complains of arthritis. Half of whatever we find will belong to my brother and we will share the other half. The claim is a good one but I warn you the work will be hard.'

'Hard work never hurt anyone,' quipped Kinqua.

'He would enjoy your skills My Li- and Kinqua's company. What do you say?'

My Li looked to Kinqua for guidance.

'What do you think?'

Kinqua replied, 'I have a strong suspicion that the events in our lives are already ordained. All we can do is accept them as they happen. Like twigs in a stream, I'll go with the flow of the current. It is your decision My Li.'

'I respect your feelings and your philosophy Kinqua but I believe I should be the one who makes the decisions that determine the direction of my life, and it is my decision that we should go with Ah Wei to his brother's claim to the south.'

'To the river to the south. So be it,' said Kinqua. 'Walk on!'

My Li, Kinqua and Ah Wei detoured around the town in the direction of Ah Wei's brother's claim. If they had continued along the road into town for another kilometre, they would have encountered a bored young Chinese, yawning and relaxing under a tree overlooking the road, as if resting before going on with his journey. But the Chinese had no journey to complete. He was one of the dwarf's look-outs, and a fully-fledged member of the local lodge of the Triad.

Although the Chinese appeared to give them scant attention, he took careful note of the number and appearance of the splinter group from the original party of fifteen Chinese that had set out from the MacArthur farm, now nearing the end of their trek and eager to enjoy themselves. His instructions however, were to be on the look-out for a large party of a dozen or more men, not the three or four who hastened past.

My Li and Kinqua were given their first indication of the degree of ill feeling between the Europeans and the orientals at the diggings when they encountered forty Chinese bearing two enormous puddling-tubs – used to decarbonise pig iron – each weighing a hundred-weight and slung on poles as thick as My Li's wrists with ten men at either end of the poles. They shuffled past in unison at a slow trot, crooning a song that gave rhythm to their steps. A European on horse-back overtook the strange rhythmically swaying assembly and, startled by the bizarre band, his horse nervously shied. The rider was almost thrown from the horse and, as he regained control, the man hoicked and spat a wad of phlegm, saying threateningly: 'You'll keep my lads. You'll keep!'

All the claims they passed had armed guards on duty and alert. They had to be careful they were not mistaken to be robbers or claim-jumpers and shot at as they plodded through the dusk towards Ah Wei's brother's claim. The European miners watched them go by with undisguised animosity in their eyes.

My Li noticed a number of Chinese picking and digging at the mounds of mullock – debris left by earlier miners. He later found out that the men were late comers, too late to the gold-fields to find a good claim, they sifted and reworked the rubbish already dug out. Working with less haste and more efficiency, they often took twice as much gold from the rejected soil than those who originally removed it.

'Where are you from?'
'Canton!'
'Honan!'
'Ningpo!'
'Foodchow!'
'Welcome!'
'Good luck.'

131

'May your ancestors smile on you.'

Greetings were constantly called and returned.

A bullock dray piled high with shoring-up planks for a mine shaft was bogged up to its rear axle and the three Chinese advanced to offer their assistance to the white teamster, but he cracked his long whip over the heads and ordered them away.

'I'll wait for my own kind!' he called after them as the Chinese tramped on.

Ah Wei's brother, Lun-Tan, welcomed Kinqua and My Li as if they were kinsmen. There were two heavy-duty canvas tents with storm flies and Ah Wei and his elder brother occupied one and gave the use of the other tent, previously used by Ah Wei's brother's partner, to My Li and Kinqua.

The sluicing was hard, dirty and repetitive toil. By the end of each day, My Lai and Ah Wei, who were given the task of barrowing the gravel from the river bank to the top of the cradle and shovelling it in at a consistent rate, were faint with fatigue.

Lun-Tan was in charge of ensuring the water flowed at the proper speed and volume and that the pipes were correctly connected. It was far less physically demanding than the work undertaken by My Li and Ah Wei but suitable for someone of Lun-Tan's age. He was a man in his mid-fifties, a decade older than Ah Wei.

Kinqua assisted Lun-Tan during the sluicing but his main role became that of chef and camp cleaner. Apart from his tiredness, My Li was content. He revelled in the routine; in being able to participate in the planning of the next day's operations; in the freedom of being his own overseer; in the pleasure of knowing that the sweat of his brow would receive monetary reward; in the amicable comradeship and the feeling that, somehow, his earlier life – including the persecution of his courtesan mother, her sad and seemingly unfair death and the malevolent murder of innocent Tiao – was becoming part of his past; albeit a tragic past.

Their evenings were agreeably passed with talks that My Li found informative and fun. Lun-Tan was a fount of knowledge about mining and the strange customs of the whites. Sometimes after a mug or two of rice wine, Lun-Tan would entertain them with facts and anecdotes he had learnt about the Europeans during his years in the Great South Land. Being Chinese, Lun-Tan was especially interested in stories about the supernatural, and the tale that most affected My Li and was Lun-Tan's vivid recounting of the legend of the Flying Dutchman; a sea captain who by an error of judgement wrecked his ship, lost his own life and the lives of his crew and was destined to forever roam the seven seas, periodically appearing out of the mist and fog in his spectral ship to warn vessels in danger; forever searching for solace and peace of mind from the torment of the past tragedy that haunted him.

The neighbouring claim on their upstream side was a company operation owned by a consortium of financiers in Melbourne. The Europeans who worked for them had installed expensive pumps and hoses. They blasted water at high pressure against the river bank, breaking up the soil and hastening their discovery of nuggets and the liberation of the gold from the detritus.

The claim on their downstream side also belonged to white men. In this instance two middle-aged prospectors who had left their town jobs, as a clerk and storekeeper respectively, to seek instant wealth at the diggings.

Although not providing them with a cash flow that might make them millionaires – far from it – their efforts at working the claim returned Lun-Tan, Ah Wei, Kinqua and My Li enough gold to live comfortably and have a small surplus, which they divided in the proportion Ah Wei had promised them. Life augured well.

One day when Kinqua and Lun-Tan returned from town with the week's supplies, Lun-Tan's best clothes were soiled with mud to his front but clean behind. His feet and arms were also caked with dried mud.

'What happened?'

'Some white men pushed Lun-Tan off the boardwalk into the street in front of the greengrocer's shop.'

'Why?'

'Because we are different. What other reason do they need? If we find gold and they don't, they get jealous. And when they become jealous they become hostile. We paid in gold-dust and the white men were watching us.'

'Did they follow you back to the claim?' Ah Wei asked anxiously, once reassured Lun-Tan had not been hurt.

'No. Nobody followed us,' Kinqua assured him.

While Lun-Tan cleaned himself and changed his clothes, My Li, Kinqua and Ah Wei sorted out the provisions they had bought, placing the meat in the wire-meshed meat-safe to protect it from flies and pouring the flour and rice into glass jars. Some of the groceries, such as the hens' eggs, were wrapped in pages of out of date English language editions of the Clarion newspaper. Below the letterpress banner title to the paper was the assertion that the Clarion spoke as the unanimous voice of the goldfield.

Kinqua did not need to know how to read English to understand the import of the cartoon on the second page of the three-day old newspaper. He handed it to My Li without a word. The cartoon portrayed an octopus with a broad oriental featured face. Its tentacles were coiled around eight helpless Europeans representing white labour, white women and various financial interests. The octopus's face wore a wicked, triumphant expression and the caption beneath it read, 'The Mongolian octopus must be stopped! The working classes should realise the serious consequences of having to compete with Tartar labour!'

The accompanying article described the Chinese as perverted moon-faced barbarians who will work for a few shillings a day and consider themselves well paid. Who can compete with them?' The article rhetorically asked, '… and who can get over the repugnance of their lank and coarse hair, slanted eyes, yellow skins and lack of beards?'

My Li was standing in the open between the tents. He glanced up from the cartoon and his eye caught that of a white miner over on their upstream neighbouring claim. It was around noon and the resting miner was reading a newspaper: the same newspaper. My Li could see the octopus cartoon. Their eyes locked and My Li found he was forced to turn away from the man's steady gaze.

CHAPTER EIGHTEEN

Weeks passed and, although the Red Poles received reports of his presence, they still did not know My Li's exact whereabouts. Chang and Yung became more and more restless and irritable. They had concluded that the dwarf's organisation was inept, and began to argue with him.

'Some look-outs!' scoffed Chang. 'Your men couldn't find a thimble on the end of their finger!'

'At least we now know that a party of fifteen arrived via the Heaven's Gate route within days of your own arrival. This My Li must have been with that party,' surmised the dwarf, anxious to defend the prowess of the men of his lodge.

'If he was, I cannot work out how we came to overtake him,' said Yung.

'We have also learnt that the party the Widow's Son accompanied split up near the crossroad. Some came into town while others made directly for the diggings!'

'…and that one of them, walking with a grey-beard, resembled My Li,' added Chang. He entwined the fingers of both hands and, tugging, cracked his knuckles as if checking their suppleness and readiness to perform the deed they had come so far to carry out.

'At least give us credit where credit is due,' wheedled the dwarf. 'It was thanks to one of my men overhearing a drunkard bragging in the saloon that we now know what we know.'

'So where is he? Perhaps I should speak to this man personally?' Chang's questions were thick with threat.

The dwarf threw up his right hand.

'I don't think that will be necessary – or wise! We have been interviewing him for two days. If he knew any more than what he has already told us, he would have revealed it by now. He knows nothing more than what we have discussed. Besides, the last time I saw him he was delirious with pain.'

'If he has told us all he knows, you had better get rid of him,' Chang said icily. 'We don't want him bleating to the authorities, do we!'

'It will be done tonight,' the dwarf assured Chang. '… and believe me gentlemen, it is only a matter of time until we find the widow's son. I am convinced he has not left the district, and we have men going from claim to claim to find him. He will not escape again. Not from this lodge. He will show up and when he does …' The dwarf leered and drew his finger slowly across his throat.

The dice player interrupted their meeting and kowtowed. 'Master, you requested that I remind you when the auction was about to begin …'

'Ah! The auction!' repeated the dwarf. 'I almost forgot! The widow's son is starting to annoy me. I have enough problems without this extra one you have brought me.'

The dwarf's comment was directed at Chang.

He stared at the dwarf without comment; a stare capable of chilling hot coals.

'Don't get me wrong though!' blustered the dwarf. 'I'm more than happy to help out …' An idea came to the dwarf. 'We must not allow our predicament to upset the balance between our yin and our yang. What we require is some humour – something light-hearted to divert us. And I think I know just the thing …'

'What do you have in mind?' asked Chang.

'Why don't you come with me and see for yourself? I am sure you will find it entertaining.'

With the dice player and the Red Poles in tow, the dwarf left the building that was his headquarters and place of livelihood. They trooped down the back streets of the Chinese quarter. Chinese men and women who saw the dwarf and his entourage approaching, fled quickly to avoid them.

The dwarf drew himself up to the extent of his short height and visibly swaggered as he saw the effect of his presence on men and women blessed with normal stature.

'They all know who I am,' the dwarf proudly told the Red Poles. 'I am a big man around here. The big man in fact.' The dwarf emphasised the word 'the'.

Grubby, snotty nosed children stopped their games in the gutters and ditches outside their back fences and watched the dwarf waddle past with rapt curiosity.

A crowd had gathered near the corrugated iron sheds at the rear of the cattle yards. The assembly numbered about sixty or seventy people. Apart from a couple of grizzled old timers, there was only one able-bodied white man present. Two thirds of the onlookers were male Chinese while the other third was comprised of middle-aged and elderly white women.

An ugly shrew in a headscarf was standing on a packing box, which raised her waist high above the heads of the crowd. There was an empty upturned beer keg in front of her and she held an ordinary claw hammer in her hand. She was apparently the auctioneer conducting the proceedings. Standing on the ground below her were the women; some were clutching their shawls around themselves as the cool of the evening came on; some were smoking pipes or jeering and exchanging lewd banter with others they knew or did not. In the midst of the women, some of whom were their own mothers, were half a dozen white female adolescents and older children. The youngest was no more than eleven years old. The oldest perhaps seventeen or eighteen.

The hag on the packing box banged her hammer on the empty beer keg for attention.

'Thank you all for coming along today, dearies,' she cried in a whining, high-pitched voice. 'We've got a lovely bunch of coconuts for sale today…'

At the word coconuts the women at her feet shrieked with amusement.

'Let's get on with it ladies. Let's have whoever is going to be first… '

A crone, with her nose showing the ravages of an advanced case of syphilis, prodded the youngest girl to her feet with a gnarled walking-stick that looked like it could also be used for other, more brutal, purposes.

'Git over there girl! Git over there where they can all git a good look at yer!'

The girl, little more than a child, did as the hag had told her.

'What is going on?' asked the Red Pole named Yung.

'It's auction day,' the dwarf replied matter of factly.

'Every first Monday of the month is auction day. Those girls are for sale to the highest bidder. There are three men to every woman on the diggings and too few of our own kind but, for a fee, some of the white women are glad to get rid of their daughters – or girls they claim are their daughters!'

The dwarf giggled. 'It is extraordinary what some of these Europeans will do for money!'

'I never knew white women would be willing to sell their own children,' Yung said, astounded. 'I have never liked the trade in bodies – whether back home or here!'

To Yung, the women present represented the dregs of European womanhood. They were not simply rough diamond types, down at heel or down on their luck or merely frumpish, rowdy or unrefined – women who might have evoked sympathy or pity for the unfortunate circumstances in which they found themselves.

These women had no redeeming qualities.

They were foul-mouthed, loathsome and vile. Yung would have walked away in disgust except for the restraining hand on his shoulder. It belonged to Chang.

'Your manners, my friend. Remember your manners and that we are far from home and dependent upon other people for their assistance. It would bring dishonour to our host if you were to offend him by turning your back on his entertainment.'

'Squeamish is he?' The dwarf was delighted. 'A Red Pole with a conscience! What will they think of next?' he asked sarcastically.

Yung chose not to answer the dwarf's taunts.

The dwarf was annoyed.

'Don't you turn your nose up!' he said testily. 'A hawk might mistake it for a timid field-mouse and, to your distress, dive on it from a great height. Hee, hee, hee!'

The dwarf laughed at his own humour and then turned to Chang. 'He is obviously not as enlightened to the ways of the world as you are.'

The dwarf felt he had found a kindred spirit in Chang and he ogled at the girls waiting to be bid for.

'What will happen next?' asked Chang.

'We will buy the more attractive ones for our brothel. The less pretty ones will be bought by the miners. We don't purchase many. We find it easier to obtain women for our brothels than do the whites. The conditions we offer are better and cleaner – and we pay more. The European whore-houses, however, are a problem. They resent our competition.'

141

'How much am I bid?' shouted the shrew on the packing box. The bids were generous and came quickly.

'Ten pounds! Ten pounds! Only ten pounds! No advance? Did I hear eleven? No advance! Going at ten. Ten only! Going, going, she's gone to the nice gentleman over there with the bad teeth!'

The gentleman with the bad teeth was pounced upon by the shrew's helpers and relieved of the contents of his wallet. Pushing the child through the throng in front of him, with one hand firmly holding her by her dress from behind, the girl's new owner left with his purchase. One of the older children was next to be offered. The girl was cross-eyed and had a downcast expression. The bidding for her was not as spirited as it had previously been. The auctioneer was quick to get rid of her and turn to her next piece of merchandise.

'Let's have you all now!' shouted the shrew with the hammer, bashing it on the keg again. 'The next girl is a beauty! She was seventeen last birthday. She's strong, straight of limb and ready for child-bearing.'

Everyone in the crowd craned their necks to get a better look at the commodity for sale.

The girl had her head bowed and her hair hung forward, obscuring her face, stained with dried tears.

'Put your head up please, dearie,' simpered the auctioneer. 'They need to see what it is they are buying with their money.'

The girl stubbornly tucked her chin into her neck.

A woman standing near to the girl tetchily said, 'Do as you're told bitch!'

The girl reluctantly lifted her head.

She had a pert nose and soulful expressive eyes that were awash with tears of dismay and fear. There was a bruise on her forehead above her right eyebrow.

She's a prime piece this one,' cried the auctioneer, getting on with her sales pitch. 'With a bit of rouge to brighten her cheeks and a new dress she's inflame the passions of a duke. Now, who will give me an offer? Who will open the bidding?'

An overweight Chinese to the rear of the crowd put up his hand.

'Thank you, sir. How much did you say? Thank you kindly Sir! That's a fair opening offer but I'm sure someone will top it!'

And someone did. As the bids rose higher the woman near the girl on auction turned to the man standing next to her and smiled broadly. The man was the only able-bodied European in the crowd. He was burlily built with muscular forearms used to heavy manual labour. He passed the pipe he was sucking to the woman who had told the girl to do as she was told. The woman accepted the pipe and they both gazed with a mixture of pride and daggers at the girl attracting the energetic bidding. They were the blacksmith and his wife from MacArthur's sheep-run, and the girl being auctioned was none other than Simone.

The winning bid was made by the dice Player.

The dwarf thought Simone would be eminently suitable for their purposes. When the blacksmith realised Simone had been bought be a Chinese, he exclaimed: 'Bought by a Chink eh! Well, at least their money is white!'

'We've done the best thing for her,' asserted his wife as she counted their money. 'She has always liked their company.'

CHAPTER NINETEEN

Following the incident when Lun-Tan was pushed headlong into the mud, Ah Wei and My Li took it upon themselves to collect their supplies and thus protect the older men from any further bullying by the Europeans. Once a week they hitched Lun-Tan's placid pony to the two wheeled trap that needed repairs they never seemed to have time to do and trundled into the town they now knew by the name of Lambing Flat.

Being a boom town, the ground on which the town stood had been grazing ground for sheep before the town sprang up in the wake of the surge of miners to the nearby diggings. Although the Chinese never numbered more than one to every ten Europeans in the colonies, and were out-numbered four or five to one on the diggings, their energy; their capacity for hard work; their innate financial acumen; their visible success and their obvious racial differences earned them the rancour of many whites – especially those who considered it their due to reap the bountiful benefits offered by the antipodean continent without working up a sweat to earn them.

The third week after My Li and Ah Wei took over the grocery supply run, they arrived on town to find a multitude of Europeans collected outside one of the Christian churches.

A man wearing a clerical collar was standing on the stone steps to the church and haranguing whoever would listen to him.

'There is disease lurking in every corner of a Chinaman's backyard! You can smell it from the street outside. The Mongol stinks of physical and moral pestilence. You only have to look at the Heathens to know they are unclean and unmanly!

At Bunabrawatha, they washed their dead in the creek! These Yellow Devils are robbing us of our gold, our livelihoods and our women! How many Tartar women do you see? They rarely bring their own women with them when they come to this country. There is scarcely two or three in the entire district yet there are thousands upon thousands of Chinamen. I have even heard tell that there is a trade in the flesh of white women in this very town! Are we just going to take it lying down? Are we going to tolerate this invasion and threat to our way of life and our decency?'

Lapping up his every word, the crowd responded with cheers and shouts of, 'no!' and 'never!'

'Are we going to stand by while these swarms of yellow locusts take over?'

'No!'

My Li and Ah Wei continued on their way. After what they had seen, their mood was subdued. When they arrived at the grocer's shop they reined in their pony, tied the reins to the verandah post and entered to choose and purchase what they required. The grocery shop was run by a Chinese and three or four Chinese were already considering items or in the process of paying for their purchases when My Li and Ah Wei walked in. While Ah Wei and My Li selected what they needed, one Chinese stared impolitely in My Li's direction. It was the man who had been resting under the tree on the approach to the town weeks earlier when My Li and Ah Wei had first arrived. The spy sent by the dwarf to

146

watch out for My Li. The man thrust whatever it was he was about to buy back on the shelf and darted out the door.

Once outside, he had doubts as to what was his best course of action and stopped. The dwarf's saloon was at the far end of the town near the joss-house. It would take him at least ten minutes to get there on his rickets affected legs. He would also have to brave the crowd of angry Europeans holding their protest meeting in front of the Christian church, and the thought that they might vent their frustrations on him filled him with dismay.

At the very least, an attempt to slip past the crowd of demonstrating whites might result in a delay in his returning with reinforcements. The widow's son might be gone by the time he could return.

'No,' he thought, it would be better if he waited and followed them to wherever the youth was living, and then return to the dwarf with the news of the wanted one's whereabouts as a fait accompli.

Neither My Li or Ah Wei noticed the young man's uncertain behaviour, or, that after having left the shop in a hurry, he was still sitting nearby when they emerged with their boxes and packages and loaded them onto the trap. After a short stop at the hardware store, the pony pulled the trap with the two men and their groceries clear of the town at an easy walk. The man spying on My Li had no problem keeping up with them. Until they were clear of town, he was able to use buildings and trees as a screen between himself and the pony cart as he followed them from a discreet distance.

Once out of town, he had to allow the pony cart to get further ahead to avoid being seen, but when they reached the diggings, the mullock mounds, machinery, tents and humpies offered ample cover, and he hurried after the fast disappearing trap. He was too late. Approaching the river and the hive of mining activities along it and within kilometres of its ore bearing banks, the trap blended in with the movements of all the other operations and, and while walking behind a bulky winch suspended above a shaft, he suddenly lost sight of the trap.

Angry at his own stupidity, he swore irritably and stood frustrated, hoping the trap might suddenly reappear and wondering what to do.

There was one thing he could not do, and that was to return to town and tell the dwarf that he had followed My Li to the diggings and then lost him. He had to find the widow's son before returning to face the dwarf.

My Li and Ah Wei released the pony from its harness and while My Li tethered, fed and watered the animal, Ah Wei took the supplies into the tents and stored them.

Lun-Tan, Kinqua, Ah Wei and My Li ate early that evening, making the most of the fresh food they had brought back from town. Plans were made for an early start at work he next day and while Lun-Tan remained to mind the claim, Ah-Wei, Kinqua and My Li went for a stroll to stretch their legs.

After an hour of admiring the sunset, their exercise aiding their digestion, exchanging greetings with other Chinese – and some white miners – they returned to camp.

All was as they had left it.

Lun-Tan was carefully applying grease to moving parts on the ore-crusher.

'It's going to have a busy day tomorrow,' he explained. 'We had better get an early start. Oh, by the way,' he said, almost as an afterthought, 'not long after you left for your walk, someone was here asking after My Li…'

'Asking after My Li?' Kinqua was the speaker. 'Who was here asking after My Li?'

Lun-Tan described the man who had followed My Li and Ah Wei out of town and back to the diggings. 'He was one of our kind; short, bowed legs and in his early twenties.

He had shifty eyes and an apology for a moustache. I have seen him in town before. He said his name was Lau.'

'What did he want?' asked My Li.

'I don't know. He did not say. I think he wanted to say hello to you. He said he had met you on the voyage to Australia. He described you quite accurately...'

Kinqua and My Li's faces registered their suspicions.

'He might be one who marched with us from MacArthur's sheep-run,' said My Li.

'I cannot recall anyone of his description,' Kinqua said. Turning to Lun-Tan, Kinqua asked, 'You say you've seen the man in town before ... before or after we came here?'

'Before.'

Kinqua's brow furrowed deeper.

'I think he is one of the shady characters who works for the dwarf,' added Lun-Tan.

'Dwarf?'

'So called because he is. He owns the brothel in Little Lotus street. I have been told that if I ever want to smoke opium and forget my aching back for a few hours, I should go to his fan-tan salon. He runs everything odious and illicit in town. If this young fellow is a friend of yours My Li, I suggest you choose your associates with greater care. If you ask me, the dwarf and his henchmen are connected with the Triad. And if they are, then they are dangerous ...'

'The Triad,' My Li said softly. 'Here in the Great South Land?'

'I have heard that if you want to set up any kind of business in Lambing Flat, you must pay the dwarf protection money. If you do not, it is more than possible your business premises might 'accidently' catch on fire.'

'I don't believe I know this man you speak of,' My Li told Lun-Tan. 'The only people who know I am here in the diggings are those who walked here with us. And the man you describe was not one of them.'

'Did you tell him My Li was here?' enquired Kinqua.

'He already knew,' replied Lun-Tan. 'He came along the river and asked for My Li at each claim. One of the white men beside us, the one My Li helped cure of his cough, pointed out our tents and he came over.'

Lun-Tan saw the worried expressions on the faces of My Li and Kinqua.

'Is anything the matter? Is something awry?'

Neither Ah Wei or Lun-Tan knew of My Li's earlier encounter with the Triad.

'There is something we should tell you,' said Kinqua. He looked at My Li. 'I think our friends should be told of your trouble ...'

An hour later, when he had finished telling Ah Wei and Lun-Tan how Tiao had been killed and the events leading up to his panic-stricken flight from the village, My Li turned to Kinqua and said, 'But I do not understand Kinqua. Why would they pursue me halfway across the world? Did I offend them so much by trying to defend my sister that they would seek me here, in a foreign country among Europeans simply to punish me?'

'I do not know. Unless ...?'

'Unless what?'

'Unless that ring you carry as a memento and reminder of your sister Tiao's final moments meant more, much more, to the Triad than we have previously assumed. Perhaps it is the ring and not you they are after?'

'The ring! It had not entered my mind that a bauble might be important to them!'

'Ring? What is the importance of a ring in all this?' asked Ah Wei.

My Li had told Ah Wei and Lun-Tan his story without mentioning that he had pocketed the ring. In comparison with the enormity of what had happened to Tiao, the

150

picking up of the ring, in My Li's opinion, paled into insignificance.

My Li explained to the brothers how, in the confusion of the fight, he had seen the ring rolling towards him in the light of the torches held aloft by Han Ying's henchmen and how he used it to defend himself.

'And you brought it with you to Australia?' asked Ah Wei.

'That is so.'

'If this man who came looking for you today, and the dwarf he works for, are indeed connected with the Triad, perhaps you could openly approach them and offer to return their ring?' speculated Lun-Tan.

'I can't,' blurted My Li. 'I gave it to the Aboriginal named Baracoona, whom we helped at Heaven's Gate.'

'Is that so,' said Kinqua with a grin. 'Well, you can't give what you don't have!'

The memory of Baracoona caused My Li to recall the Aboriginal's insistence that one of the two orientals who had poisoned his clan had had a scarred nose. And the recollection of a man with a mutilated nose brought a rush of horrific images gushing into his mind: Tiao's last despairing cry for him to save himself; the bloody flash of the man's sword in the lantern and torchlight; the alarm and terror of his night flight through the paddy-fields and the close encounter with his pursuers from the ditch – that might have so easily resulted in his death.

Was it all because of the ring thought My Li? If so, had he passed a poisoned chalice to Baracoona?

'Baracoona gave me what he called a tjurunga – a talisman, and I gave him the ring in return,' explained My Li, beginning to comprehend the possibility that the Triad might be determined to pursue him to his grave.

151

'So there is an Aboriginal wandering the wilderness wearing a ring the Triad possible pursued My Li across the Southern Sea to regain!' marvelled Ah Wei. 'The ways of the world are indeed wonderful!'

'Indeed!' echoed Kinqua. 'But if what we surmise is in fact true, then My Li is in peril from the Triad even here in the Great South Land.'

'What do you think they will do?' My Li asked Kinqua.

Kinqua arched his eyebrows.

'I am not an expert in the ways of assassins but even if you still possessed the ring, I don't believe these people are the type who would graciously accept it back and tip you for going out of your way to return it. Of more importance, perhaps, is what you intend to do?'

'I don't know. What would you advise Kinqua?'

'Sometimes the sound of pursuing feet is merely the echo of our own footsteps. Let us seek out this man Lau and his master the dwarf and, without revealing our own hand, do some sleuthing of our own. If the Triad is truly here, among us on the gold-fields, it means sadness and sorrow for this Great South Land.'

The man known as Lau, who had traced My Li to Lun-Tan's claim on the diggings, ran back to town as fast as his short, bowed legs could carry him. He gave the coded knock on the door to the rear of the dwarf's salon and was led through the gambling den, past the doors with opium smoke wafting out from underneath them until he was ushered into the presence of the dwarf.

The dwarf, with the assistance of the two women with him when the Red Poles first arrived, was entertaining guests and discussing the state of the old country, which he had not seen for some years, when Lau was brought before the seated men. Lau kowtowed.

'I have found him Master. I have found the widow's son!'

The Red Poles leant forward expectantly.

Chang smirked in triumph and his face suddenly resembled that of a gargoyle frightening away demons from a Christian church, rather than any human being.

'Where is he?'

Knowing the importance that had been placed on finding My Li and having some idea of the scale of the dwarf's resources that had been directed at finding him, Lau had been contemplating a rich reward for his efforts. An underling of the lowest grade of Triad membership, Lau, like everybody else, knew who the strangers with his master were, but he was not cognisant with the Red Poles' mission – or of its importance.

Now the information he had so assiduously accumulated was being demanded from him with less grace then someone asking street directions. Lau preened knowingly. If he was clever, so he thought, he could at the very least barter his hard earned information for a reasonable reward.

He had not reckoned with Chang. As Lau procrastinated in giving his reply, the Red Pole stood up and, taking one lone stride to bring himself within striking distance, he lashed out with his right leg. His foot connected with Lau's nose and the crack as it broke and shifted to one side of his face was audible to all those in the room.

'Where is he?' repeated Chang. 'I don't want to have to ask again.'

Even the dwarf was impressed by Chang's impetuous recourse to violence and he went pale as blood freely drenched the front of Lau's shirt. Holding his broken nose as if it might fall off, Lau quickly gabbled out My Li's whereabouts to prevent Chang taking offence again and dealing him another sickening blow.

When Lau had finished, and while he sat snivelling on the floor, Chang turned to the dwarf and with total disrespect to his host demanded, 'Six of your men – and good ones - armed and ready to leave in ten minutes.'

The dwarf's mouth was agape.

He stared at Lau and then back at Chang, bemused by the abruptness with which his evening of leisure and repose had been transformed – and annoyed by Chang's attitude and what he saw was unnecessary aggression.

Yung, too, was irked by Chang's sudden resort to force, and he noticed that Chang was wearing the same grin that Yung had seen on his face when the poisoned Aboriginals had been convulsing in their death throes at the gorge.

The big Red Pole seemed to take excessive pleasure from his work.

CHAPTER TWENTY

When My Li and Kinqua ventured into Lambing Flat, yet another European was inciting racial hatred from the steps of the church. With his arms folded across his chest and his head nodding in grave agreement with what was being said stood the cleric, giving tacit support to the torrent of bigotry pouring out of the speaker's mouth.

'We even allow a heathen temple in our midst!' cried a bearded demagogue, pointing in the direction of the joss-house. 'It is there that the yellow bastards are making their plans to take us over! For that is their ultimate intention! Do you want to be taken over by the Chinese?'

'No!' roared his audience of respectable citizenry, tradesmen and professionals, their wives and the dissatisfied Europeans who wanted to find gold without doing any labour to obtain it. The demagogue had cleverly manipulated his audience into a state of intense hostility to anything Chinese, and their hate was tangible as My Li and Kinqua hurried by, keeping to the shadows and out of the way of the ugly-mooded crowd.

As far as My Li was aware, the only gatherings that took place in the Chinese temples were those to recite the scriptures, chant the litanies and to entertain the monks on

155

the seventh day. It did not occur to him that those same ritual events also provided a focal point for white racial discontent.

The Chinese had become accustomed to the campaign of vilification and, although the atmosphere that night was more vehement, more hysterical and rowdier than usual, My Li and Kinqua thought nothing was out of the ordinary, and they stuck to their plan to reconnoitre the fan-tan saloons and seedy Chinese dens of inequity in the hope of spotting the man Lau – described to them by Lun-Tan – or even the man with the mutilated nose, whom Baracoona told them had committed the atrocity against his tribesmen and whose tracks had led towards Lambing Flat. A sighting of the man with the scarred nose would confirm the presence of the Triad in the Great South Land, and My Li's need to be concerned for his personal well-being.

'Are you sure you will remember him? It is a long time since you last saw him?'

'I would recognise him anywhere,' My Li asserted.

'And if we do see him?'

'Then I will know for sure that the Triad is hunting for me like the white men when they chase foxes with their dogs.'

Although Kinqua had little faith in the idea, My Li still held hope of finding a way of contacting Lau or the scarred man – if he was indeed on the diggings – by third party or by note, and of negotiating the return of the ring in exchange for a guarantee of his safety.

'If that is actually what they are after,' said Kinqua. 'But how will you find Baracoona if it is what they want?'

'The tjurunga,' replied My Li. 'That is why Baracoona gave it to me.'

My Li had put on the European style trousers and boots that he had received while working on the sheep-run to try and make himself look more like an old-hand miner than a new boy to the diggings. He also rubbed dirt across his clean face to add to the image. Although night, Kinqua wore his straw hat with its brim tugged down. My Li put on a low peaked Dutchman's cap borrowed from Lun-Tan.

The first saloon they entered was in the vicinity of the church – and of the growing numbers of European people congregating outside. The atmosphere inside the saloon was far from frivolous. The Chinese drinking and gambling were subdued. They perpetually cast uneasy glances in the church's direction whenever they heard a new vocal eruption of approval or satisfaction with what was being said. Their repressed fear and a sense of impending doom was palpable. But My Li and Kinqua were so preoccupied, they did not notice.

The next place they went into was an unlicensed grog shop serving watered down black naval rum. With his hands pressed into his pockets and his shoulders hunched, more with tension than a deliberate attempt at disguise, My Li, with Kinqua at his side, sauntered into the bar. Business was bad. There were fewer than twenty men in a room that could accommodate over a hundred. The pair went in and out of another four premises, some busier than others, before finally, unbeknown to either of them, entering the fan-tan saloon owned by the dwarf.

The dwarf's saloon was doing better trade than the others My Li and Kinqua had previously visited that night. A success possibly to do with the saloon being further away from where the white people were meeting – but it was most likely more to do with what was going on in the back rooms.

My Li and Kinqua bought drinks of sam-soo and found an unoccupied bench tucked away in an under-lit corner. From there they could watch whoever came in or went out the street door, through which they had just entered. The room was filled but not packed. The occupants were mainly men and nearly all Chinese. The few women present were white and garishly rouged. They all wore flounced full-length dresses with low-cut bodices.

Both Kinqua and My Li were tired. They had worked a full day at the claim before setting out and had already visited five establishments – buying drinks in three as a pretext for their presence – before their arrival at the dwarf's fan-tan saloon. Now they were flagging and the novelty and excitement of their excursion into town was rapidly wearing off. They sat sipping their drinks and studying the faces around them.

It was Kinqua who drew My Li's attention to the fact there was more traffic going in and out a door to the rear of the room than through the door opening onto the street.

He nudged My Li's arm and the friends soon saw the reason for the anomaly.

They observed that every now and then, one of the women, invariably accompanied by one of the male customers, got up and went through the door at the rear of the room.

The first woman to take her customer through returned without him some twenty minutes later.

The second woman to do so had still not returned after half an hour. Other men went through the door by themselves; some to re-emerge while others did not. Some men, whom My Li and Kinqua had not noticed in the public room, came through the door and immediately left the building; others remained and mingled.

It was obvious to My Li and Kinqua that the door at the rear of the room led to the unadvertised delights available on the premises.

'If either the man known as Lau or the man-with-the-scarred nose are here, then they are most probably the other side of that door,' My Li thought aloud.

From their position in the corner, whenever the rear door opened and shut, My Li was able to catch glimpses of what was beyond it.

From what little he could see, it appeared there was an inner room, more resplendently decorated than the spartan public area where they now sat.

Once, before the door shut, he saw three or four men seated at a table. They were playing cards like many in the public area. But My Li gained the impression the game going on in the inner room was far more serious than where they sat.

'What say we take a look in there, Kinqua?'

Kinqua pursed his lips doubtfully.

'I fear we might be pushing out luck too far. Even if the applause persists, the lion tamer does not stand with his head between the jaws of the lion for too long.'

My Li was mulling over the risk and Kinqua had just begun to suggest they should call it a night and go back to the claim when the door opened and the second woman they had noticed go through it returned.

She was a woman in her forties. In her younger years she would undoubtedly have been pretty but an excessive alcohol intake had created a patchwork of reddish capillary veins on her nose and cheeks that even her heavy make-up could not hide, giving her a ruddy, blowsy appearance. As she pushed open the door she was adjusting her dress and patting her hair into place with her right hand. But it was not that woman who caught My Li's attention. The woman's left hand was firmly gripped to the elbow of a younger woman, who from her obvious reluctance, did not want to be in the public room. She steered the younger woman to the table she had earlier left with a customer to go through the rear door.

The women's backs were turned to My Li and Kinqua but they were able to observe what ensued. The blowsy woman introduced her unwilling companion to the men sitting at the table she had left earlier.

One of the men grinned lasciviously and patted the empty seat that the older woman had vacated beside him. The younger girl demurred and became interested in the floor.

For a moment My Li felt there was something vaguely familiar about her stance. He noted she was similarly dressed to the older woman and that her nails were painted red; that her hair had been swept up into a Madam Pompadour hairstyle and was held in place with long hairpins. The older woman was explaining something to the men.

She gestured at the girl and then to the pipe one of the men was furiously puffing at, substantially contributing to the blue haze of smoke that hung under the ceiling. When the older woman finished whatever it was she had to say, the man with the lascivious grin said something to the younger woman that made the back of her neck blush beneath its layer of powder. The man rose from his chair and the younger woman turned and walked to the rear door, through which she had entered moments earlier. The man followed her but had to quicken his stride to prevent the door closing in his face, as the young woman did not slacken her pace and wait for him to accompany her. As she turned side on to My Li and Kinqua to exit, My Li saw her in profile and a pang of recognition went through him.

He had no doubt about her identity.

'It's Simone!' My Li whispered to Kinqua.

CHAPTER TWENTY-ONE

'How did she get here?'

'I don't know how she got here but I'm certain she isn't here because she wants to be! Wait for me Kinqua. I am going to follow her!'

'I'll come with you!'

'No! If we have to leave in a hurry, I can run faster than you, but I could not leave you behind. It is better I go alone. If I am not back in half an hour, wait for me by the track to Lun-Tan's claim!'

My Li stood up, and feigning a bravado he did not feel, he sauntered between the patrons' tables to the doorway to the inner rooms as if he was used to using it. The door opened at the twist of his hand and nobody shouted at him to stop. With a quick glance to where Kinqua sat, barely breathing and as still as a statue, My Li shut the door to the public area behind him.

The door opened into a corridor.

Opposite the door was another door. My Li saw that his glimpses into the other room had depended upon both doors being open simultaneously. To his left along the corridor was a man My Li assumed to be a guard or a bouncer.

He had his back towards My Li and was facing a door that, from My Li's limited knowledge of the layout of the building, could only have opened into a side alley.

The door had an upper panel that swung open inwards and the guard was talking heatedly with someone on the other side of the door.

A man was demanding admittance but the bouncer was refusing to let him in. My Li's conviction that the door led outside was confirmed, and he filed its location in his memory. While the bouncer was preoccupied, My Li opened the door opposite and walked through. He found himself in a large room with a stage at one end like a meeting-room or hall – the same room the Red Poles had been led into on their arrival when they first met the dwarf.

As when the Red Poles passed through it, about forty men and four woman, three white and one Chinese, were present. My Li had surmised that the stakes at the games going in at the tables in the inner room were high but he was amazed at the amount of cash lying on the green baize. Once in the room My Li looked for Simone. But she was not there. My Li did not know what to do with himself and curious eyes were already looking in his direction. Then he saw the door on the other side of the room. My Li strode towards it, again waiting for the cry to halt that did not come.

The gamblers either totally ignored him or looked up quizzically as he passed before returning their concentration to their games and their betting.

My Li let himself into the corridor with four doors either side and the doorway leading to the dwarf's private room at the far end of it. My Li opened the nearest door. The room was lit by an oil lamp and was small and bare apart from three benches, one along each length of wall. On the benches were palliasses, bolsters for head-rests, a threadbare blanket and three recumbent men.

On the floor beside two of the men and on the palliasse next to the third, were trays strewn tapers and matches and bearing earthenware bottles with wicks. On one of the trays was the thick pipe through which its user had been inhaling opium. The pipes the other men had been using were clutched firmly in their hands.

A single joss-stick, almost all burnt to ash, was stuck into a crack in the windowless wall and the greasy, perfumed odour of opium pervaded the room so strongly that, as he held open the door, it welled out from within and made My Li involuntarily sniff.

Only one of the men was sufficiently in control of his senses to take notice of My Li's appearance. He slowly turned his head and stared unblinkingly and blankly at the intruder with half-closed, heavy lidded eyes.

The other two opium smokers remained staring at the blackened ceiling. My Li gently shut the door.

Only opening the door to the second room a few centimetres wise, My Li put his eye to the gap. Inside the room was a double bed, on which one of the white whores he had minutes earlier seen in the public room, was kneeling, still dressed, astride her client.

My Li managed to shut the door again without her knowing it had ever opened.

My Li turned to the other side of the hallway.

The next room he tried had an empty bed. He was about to try the door-handle beyond it when the door at the end of the corridor – the dwarf's – opened slightly and let a line of light spill along the unilluminated corridor.

A hand grasped the door and My Li could hear voices arguing. Someone was about to come out and find him in the corridor. My Li slipped into the empty room and, squeezing it closed, leant, heart pounding against the door.

My Li waited inside the dark tomb of a room for what felt to him like eternity, while the speakers made references to 'pushy Red Poles' and then said their farewells. The voices rose in volume and then My Li heard the sound of the door shutting and the latch catching as it closed. Footsteps came towards the door he was hidden behind and, to My Li's relief, continued beyond it.

When he heard another door close, My Li punted that the path was clear and let himself back into the corridor. There was no-one there. My Li renewed his position at the fourth door and turned the knob.

The room was similar to the first room My Li looked into, with the benches arranged for the convenience of opium smokers. This room also had occupants. On the bench against the wall to My Li's left stretched the man with the lecherous grin; the man who had followed Simone from the public area.

The man's feet were towards My Li and his head was resting on a bolster. The same kind of tray My Li had seen in the first room lay on the floor by the man's head and, in one hand, he was holding the stem of the pipe he had moments earlier finished drawing on. The wick on the earthernware bottle was still alight and grotesque shadows hurled themselves across the walls encouraged by its fluttering flame.

A figure was steadying the pipe for the man with one hand and holding a used pellet of opium, which he had inhaled, on a long pin with her other. She slowly turned her head to the door.My Li found himself staring at Simone. My Li raised his forefinger to his lips.

The man had not heard the door open and did not move. Simone remained squatting on the floor, holding the man's pipe, two pellets of molasses-like raw opium on the tray beside her.

Unfazed by My Li's unexpected appearance, Simone returned My Li's gaze questioningly but without recognition.

My Li realised she had no idea who he was. Her eyes were wide and regarded him calmly. From his experience as an apothecary, it was obvious to My Li that Simone had been affected by the drug she was administering. It looked to My Li as if it was her job to mould and hold the opium pellets on the pin over the flame while the customer took in the smoke. It would be impossible for her not to absorb some of the hallucinatory fumes.

The man lying on the bench let go of the pipe and his hand flopped loosely as the opium took effect. Simone placed the pipe on the tray and rose to her feet. 'I did it right. He didn't lose any and I didn't waste it. See! There are two pellets left.'

'Simone! It's me! My Li!'

Simone had to think hard.

'My Li? My Li?' she repeated. But then the name sank into her befuddled brain and her face lit up brighter than the [insert 'dully glowing'] lamp suspended above her head. She rushed forward and hugged My Li. My Li returned her embrace and pushed the door closed behind them with his heel.

The opium smoker lifted his head at the sound of the door shutting and, on seeing My Li and Simone, leered and said, 'Ain't love grand!' before closing his eyes and resting his head back on the bolster – slipped into a stupor.

Simone and My Li, released each other.

'He's out of his senses,' whispered Simone. 'No-one will disturb us for a few minutes. How did you know where to find me?'

'I didn't. Kinqua and I were sitting in the public area and saw you. I followed you back here. How did you get involved in this place?'

'MacArthur fired my father.'

165

'What for?'

'He killed one of the Chinese. After you and Kinqua left he hated your kind worse than before. One day the Chinaman helping him in the forge, pumping the bellows, didn't work them as fast as he wanted and my father beat him to death.

MacArthur decided not to hand him over to the authorities as he would have been charged with murder. But the Chinese workers all went on strike until something had to be done. MacArthur was finally forced to ask him to leave as there was so much bad feeling and the Chinese were refusing to work.'

My Li waited for Simone to continue.

'My father determined to try his luck on the gold-fields. We have only been here a few weeks.'

'But you? In this place? How?' My Li struggled to express himself in English.

Simone hung her head.

'My parents sold me to the owner, the dwarf.' Then she looked My Li in the eye. 'Can you believe it? They sold me like a sheep or lump of meat! The dwarf's people made me smoke opium but one of the girls here tipped me off to what they were up to. They encourage you to smoke the drug until you are addicted and then they know you'll never try and run away from your source. So I've always pretended to take in more than I had. They taught me how to prepare it for smoking and I have to give it to whoever comes in and pays for it. That way I would be constantly around the drug – which they hoped would hasten my dependency. Once hooked, they will make me work as a whore to earn my opium. That's what happened to the girl I talked to. They beat her for telling me. I've been waiting for the right moment to run away. But what are you and Kinqua doing here? This isn't the kind of place I would have thought you would come to?'

'Nor I you Simone. We think someone is trying to find me. Some people with whom I had trouble in China. We fear they have followed me here. A man with a scarred nose. We came here tonight to see if we could find a man with a mutilated nose.'

Simone mentally grappled with what My Li was telling her.

'They are here!' she exclaimed, remembering the men who had come to the MacArthurs' kitchen while she was shut in the cold store. 'The man with the scarred nose is here in this very building. He and another man who goes everywhere with him have been here since I have! Everyone is frightened of them! It is rumoured they are hired killers brought out by the dwarf to do his bidding. But I've noticed they take little notice of the dwarf. He does what they want him to do. I've been keeping out of their way since I was brought here in case they recognised me but they wouldn't have a clue I was the same person as the one they met at MacArthur's. Not under all this!'

Simone indicated her make-up and giggled.

'Then we have found out what we came here for. It's time to leave.'

'The dwarf has cut-throats everywhere. Do you have a plan?'

'No. But it will be easy…' said My Li. 'We will walk into the public area as if you are helping a satisfied customer to his seat, collect Kinqua and leave.' My Li took Simone's hand and, as the man on the bench murmured contentedly, he opened the door into the corridor.

167

CHAPTER TWENTY-TWO

A few days later, the *Sydney Morning Herald* published an eyewitness account of the events that began on the night My Li and Kinqua ventured into Lambing Flat in their attempt to find out whatever they could about the man Lau, who had come snooping around Lun-Tan's claim, and his master, the dwarf.

By a quirk of synchronicity, their visit coincided with the social unrest that has since become renowned as the Lambing Flat Riots. The newspaper's correspondent wrote the following report:

> *Armed with pick-handles, whips and revolvers, the men marched on the Chinese camps, burning them to the ground and pursuing the terrified Chinese. The Chinamen were knocked down and robbed, their swags taken from them and cast into the river. Chinese stores were broken into and looted during scenes of ruffianly behaviour, unmanly violence, and unbound rapacity. They charged into the camps where the Chinese were industriously plying their callings and interfering with no-one. As they neared the encampments, the mobs broke into a run, and with yells and hoots, hunted and whipped the Chinamen off, knocking them down with the butt ends of their whips, galloping after them on horse-back, and using the most cruel torture upon the defenceless creatures;*

169

in many cases pulling out their pigtails by the roots. The white men rifled tents and buildings of all their gold, then set fire to them. One poor creature, a white woman married to a Chinaman, was maltreated by the mob, and her infant, lying in its cradle, narrowly escaped – as the wretches set fire to the cradle. Unarmed and defenceless, the unresisting Chinese were struck down in the most brutal manner. Some attackers cut off their pigtails with the scalp attached! Yet another unfortunate Chinese was dragged to a clump of trees near his camp where the miners cut off his pigtail, tied his hands with it, and made him stand on a bucket against a tree. They then nailed his ears to the tree and kicked the bucket from under his feet. He was left hanging there until released the following day.

The riots began when the anti-Chinese crowd My Li and Kinqua had seen earlier in the evening dispersed after their meeting.

The more respectable citizens and their womenfolk went home, but the remainder, including the layabout elements – composed of single men; miners who had not found their fortune and who resented those who had; now worked up into a pitch of racial hatred. They fanned out from the meeting, collecting other riff-raff as they went. They were intent on venting their resentment and hostility on the objects of their vilification. The unruly mob, armed themselves with whatever came to hand and headed for the Chinese end of town.

With a growl like an angry animal, the mob marched to the Chinese temple. Forcing the lock to the carved double doors they burst inside, ripping down drapes and tapestries and tearing up placards bearing symbolic ideographs. Piling anything flammable on the floor, they tipped the contents of an oil lamp over the pile and set fire to it.

Within seconds the flames had spread to the timber panelled walls. Within minutes the building was engulfed and the raucous cheering mob descended on the Chinese quarter, breaking into bars and stealing anything alcoholic they could get their hands on. They looted Chinese owned shops and left them ablaze and, finally, entered the fan-tan saloons in a savage search of human prey. Any Chinese they caught were beaten and robbed; women in the brothels raped and beaten; especially white women who were considered to have betrayed their colour and consorted with the Yellow Men.

The swelling clamour that accompanied the approach of the mob and the splintering crashes, thumps and individual yells of fear and exultation as groups of drunken and unruly men smashed their way into the dwarf's premises were clearly audible to My Li as he stood in the open doorway. At that moment Kinqua burst into the corridor.

'The Europeans are killing our kind! Hurry! We must hurry and get out of here!' urged Kinqua as he set eyes on My Li. My Li tugged at Simone's arm and all three were standing in the corridor when the door to the dwarf's inner sanctum opened, spreading light down the length of the corridor and even on the faces of the three friends standing frozen with surprise and shock. Coming out of his lair to investigate the cause of the commotion, the dwarf came face to face with My Li. The bewildered dwarf looked from Simone to Kinqua to My Li.

'He is obviously the dwarf,' said My Li.

Simone nodded.

Kinqua said, 'My Li! We must go! Now!'

'My Li,' repeated the dwarf. 'My Li! The widow's son? Here? The amazed dwarf put his head back inside his room and called for his bodyguard.

'The widow's son is here! Get him! Quickly! We'll show those pretentious, posturing Red Poles! The Five Ancestors will reward us richly!'

The bodyguard emerged from the dwarf's chamber and pushed past him.

'Take Simone, Kinqua!' called My Li as he blocked the bodyguard's advance. 'We'll meet where we agreed! You know the place!'

Kinqua tugged at Simone. Still affected by the drug, Simone was momentarily confused and torn by a sense of loyalty to stay with My Li.

'Go with Kinqua!' pleaded My Li.

'Please Simone!'

Turning twice to see if My Li might be following, Simone ambled sedately along the corridor with Kinqua.

'Hold him! Hold him!' chanted the dwarf as My Li grappled with the bodyguard. Heaven will reward you!'

The bodyguard was skilled and My Li beat a desperate fighting retreat along the corridor, trying to ensure the bodyguard did not get a grip on him while buying time for Simone and Kinqua to get clear of the building. But the bodyguard was more powerful and with the dwarf urging him on, the bodyguard managed to grab hold of My Li's miner's shirt.

'Got him!' shrieked the dwarf. 'But what's going on out there!' he added, suddenly aware of the uproar outside and in the public area of the building.

As the bodyguard twisted My Li's arm up behind his back, making him powerless to resist further, three white men opened the door into the corridor.

'Here, look, they're beating the shit out of one of our blokes!'

'Bastards!'

'Let's get them!'

The three miners launched themselves at the bodyguard. The dwarf turned and scampered back into his room, slamming and then locking the door. The bodyguard was trying to hold onto My Li and keep away from the miners who had come to My Li's rescue, thinking he was European because of the clothes he had chosen to wear into town. As the bodyguard tried to protect himself from the flurry of blows aimed at him, My Li was able to wrest himself from the man's grip and, leaving his assailant to his fate, flee along the corridor.

My Li ran into the room occupied by the high stake gamblers when he followed Simone. He was confronted by bedlam. There were Chinese fighting to protect their winnings from Europeans intent on stealing their money from them. There were white men collecting bottles of liquor and anything else that took their fancy. There were bloodied Chinese groaning in agony on the floor.

A European was standing under an oil lamp and holding a nugget up to the light to examine its value more closely. A spreading puddle of sticky red was oozing out from under a Chinese lying prone on the floor at My Li's feet. A shovel with a sharpened and blood-stained blade had been tossed into a corner, having done the work it was not designed for.

The green baize topped tables were overturned and ripped; glasses were smashed and shiny slivers reflected the lamp light.

Keeping his head down, My Li crossed the room. The white men were so intent on robbing and wanton destruction they ignored him, assuming he was of their own. My Li reached the door on the far side of the room and went into the corridor. The door into the public area was open. It was packed with white men and badly beaten Chinese.

Similar scenes to those in the gambling room met his eyes and My Li realised he had little hope of reaching the main street that way without being seen to be Chinese.

The door into the side lane, with the panel that could be removed to check who was knocking, was shut and unattended. My Li sprang towards it and, flinging it open, leapt into the alley beyond it; straight into another group of miners. They were armed with a frightening collection of weapons; a whip, a pick-handle and knives.

'Going somewhere Chink?'

My Li could not recall later which one of the men first struck him. He never saw the blow coming. But he felt its impact, and that of those that followed. My Li was beaten to his knees. One man was hitting him about the back of his head and shoulders with the butt of the whip. Another European kicked him in the ribs with the toe of his hobnailed blucher boots. A flailing blow from the hilt of the whip knocked off My Li's cap.

'Stop it!' cried a white man, forcing his way through those intent on doing damage to My Li. 'Stop it I say!' The newcomer pulled the man with the whip away from My Li.

'What? Who do you think you are?'

'Leave him alone! This one once saved my life.'

'So what?'

'A Chink lover eh?' sneered the man with the pick-handle poised for the coup de grace over My Li's unprotected head.

'Drop it!' insisted the newcomer. 'I owe this one my life!'

My Li was dazed and disorientated. He looked up from where he was sprawled in the dirt to see who it was protecting him. The man was young but the only clue to his identity was the belaying pin he had stuck in his belt.

'I don't give a damn,' said another of My Li's attackers, a pot-bellied man with a stubble of grey beard.

'He is yellow! He is Chinese and he is dead!'

The man drew a pistol with a revolving chamber from his trouser pocket and thumbed back the firing hammer until it was cocked. My Li found himself looking up at the octagonal barrel of the pistol. There was a flash as the pistol discharged and the report deafened My Li's ears and left them ringing. Suddenly the revolver was lying on the ground in front of him and its owner was hopping from one foot to the other, clutching his right hand, which had been holding the pistol, and yelping with pain.

My Li's protector placed himself between My Li and his assailants. The belaying pin he had moments earlier cracked across the knuckles of the pot-bellied man still grasped in his hand.

My Li had still not recognised the young man and he struggled to work out who his benefactor might be. The young man holding the belaying pin bent and scooped up the pistol. 'Now clear off or I'll hoist you all from the nearest yard-arm!'

The nautical term rang a familiar bell in My Li's brain. But he still could not recall who his young rescuer might be.

His benefactor was now armed with the pistol as well as the belaying pin and My Li's attackers backed off but remained scowling and threatening from a safe distance. My Li groaned and forced himself to stand up. His benefactor assisted him.

'You don't know who I am, do you?'

My Li looked at the handsome young face framed by fair hair. The newcomer was younger than My Li. He grinned impishly and pointed with the belaying pin to a smallpox scar on his forehead.

'That was one you missed! I was the midshipman of the Dayspring. You saved my life and tied me to the bunk to stop me scratching my sores. You were like an angel of mercy to me. Your face is engraved on my memory! I knew it was you as soon as I saw you.'

My Li recalled the incident. 'The midshipman!'

'That's right. Now come on. These fellows might get their confidence back in a minute and decide to have another go at you.'

'Were you with them,' My Li indicated the men who had attacked him.

'Yes. I deserted the Dayspring after her return trip to China to come to the diggings. I was sharing a claim with these men.'

The midshipman helped My Li hobble down the alley. The shipmates watched them go.

'Don't come back, Mark!'

'You'd better go back to sea mate! You're not welcome with us after this.'

'Come near us again Chink lover and you'll get the rest of what he should have got!'

'Leave me,' said My Li. 'Your friends will turn on you.'

'I've already turned against them. By the way, my name is Mark.'

'Thank you, Mark.'

'Which way should we go? Do you have somewhere to go?'

'That way!' said My Li, indicating the direction of Lun-Tan's claim, and with the white midshipman called Mark holding him up, they stumbled away from the murderous mayhem of Lambing Flat. Behind them, screaming Chinese ran from berserk whites armed with axes and firearms. Buildings were ablaze and horses, dogs, cattle and chickens neighed, barked, lowed and cackled in fright and fled from the noise and the flames.

CHAPTER TWENTY-THREE

'…and so I deserted.'

Mark the midshipmen finished telling My Li how he came to be nearby when My Li was attacked. 'I couldn't stand the thought of another hellish voyage with that abominable man.'

'I thought you were related to Captain Middleton?'

'Only by the marriage of one of my three sisters. I was at sea long before he became family. I went to sea when I was twelve years old. I was never keen on being on the same ship but my sister was enthused by the idea and I went along with it.'

'He seemed very concerned when you were ill.'

Mark snorted. 'My sister would have been exceedingly upset if Middleton had returned to tell her favourite and only brother had died aboard his pestilence ridden ship! The man is a monster! You wouldn't believe how bad he became. The voyage after the one you were on, he gave instructions for a wooden triangle to be erected on the foc's'le to tie the poor fellows against while they were being flogged…'

'His Chinese passengers?'

'No! The seamen! His crew! After that I jumped ship and came to the diggings. So did half the crew of the Dayspring! I teamed up with those fellows you ran into last night purely on a commercial basis, of course. As they say, you can choose your friends but not your business associates. I would not normally have associated with the likes of them but these are not normal times, are they?'

My Li, Kinqua, Simone and Mark were nearly in sight of Lun-Tan's claim. Kinqua and Simone had reached safety unharmed and were waiting hidden among the bushes beside the track back to the diggings. My Li and Mark had crept along the track in the dark. It was pitch black but there was a lot of activity as marauding white men hunted for Chinese victims. My Li and Mark were constantly forced to leave the track and hide whenever groups of white miners were encountered. Their lamps and blazing torches bobbing in the darkness unpleasantly reminded My Li of his last night in his native village. He felt world weary wondered if there was any corner of the globe that offered refuge from persecution and oppression.

'Kinqua! Simone! It's My Li! It's alright! I'm with a friend! You can come out now!'

My Li had to hoarsely repeat himself three or four times before there was an answering call from Kinqua. There was a lengthy delay until some bushes rustled beside the track and Kinqua loomed out of the night with a sheepish grin across his face. He put his arms around My Li and gladly embraced him.

'I wasn't expecting company,' Kinqua pointed out. 'And I had to be sure whoever was with you had our best interests at heart. Who is this?' he asked, staring at Mark.

My Li re-introduced Kinqua to the midshipman from the Dayspring.

Kinqua then said, 'I told Simone to stay hidden in case you had been forced to come here. Having Mark with you made it appear to be a trap. I'll go and get her.'

'We will come with you,' said My Li. 'I think it will be safer for us to wait a few hours before returning to the claim. There are too many white men coming and going along the track.'

Kinqua took My Li and Mark to where Simone was crouching in the scrub. Simone was introduced to Mark and, while the hue and cry died down and the shouts of men using the track became less frequent, the four outcasts, each proscribed or estranged from sections of their own communities, related their tales to each other.

In the pre-dawn – piccaninny light, as Baracoona called it – they set out on the final few kilometres to Lun-Tan's claim. When they arrived at the river, the early morning light revealed Lun-Tan's claim to be a ruin of smouldering equipment and charred canvas. My Li and Mark ran ahead of Simone and Kinqua.

Ah Wei was sitting among the burnt debris of his brother's claim. An ominously shaped bundle with a blanket over it lay on the scorched ground beside him. At their approach, Ah Wei slowly looked up to see who was coming. His head was swathed in a makeshift bandage, stained dark with blood. It sat on his skull like a turban. But it wasn't the extra weight that made his movements slow with lassitude. Ah Wei's eyes revealed a crushed and stricken spirit.

My Li and Mark were brought to a halt by the sight.

Ah Wei put a hand on the bundle by his side. 'Lun-Tan is dead.'

Forgetting his own injuries and soreness, My Li knelt beside the blanket covered form and lifted one corner. Lun-Tan lay beneath it, his eyes closed and his face strangely composed and peaceful despite his violent death.

Undoubtedly violent, as My Li could see from the bruises to Lun-Tan's features and, as his head was angled to one side, from the terrible wound just below and behind the ear. My Li lowered the blanket and placed his right hand over Ah Wei's.

'What happened here, Ah Wei?'

'We were asleep,' Ah Wei, still surprised by the night's events.

'They dragged us from our tent and did this...'

Ah Wei's voice choked with emotion.

A boot scuffed gravel and My Li, Mark and Ah Wei looked up to see some of the white miners from the neighbouring claim owned by the company in Melbourne standing stony faced, arms folded across their chests, just inside the boundary of their own claim.

'Bastards,' breathed Mark, not so loud that the watching men might have heard. The Europeans did not hear him but Ah Wei did.

'It wasn't the white men who did this! Oh no! It was Chinese from town. The man called Lau who was looking for you yesterday was with them My Li! They were looking for you!'

'For me?'

Ah Wei nodded his bandaged head.

'The man Lau had a broken nose. He kept pointing to it and saying it was because of you, My Li. That it was your fault he was here.'

'If it wasn't for the white men on the next claim, I would have been killed too.'

Ah Wei indicated the watching miners.

'They came over to see what was going on and when the men from town realised you weren't here, they left. But the miners were too late to help Lun-Tan. One of Lau's men took great delight in beating him. "Where is the widow's son," he kept demanding? I tried to stop him but others held me. There were at least seven of them. Finally

180

he hit Lun-Tan with our axe... he had a scar here, at the bottom of his nose... he also wanted to know about the ring you told us about. We told him it was not here, and that you did not have it – but he refused to listen.'

Ah Wei pointed to where the man's scar had been but My Li could not bring himself to look at Ah Wei. My Li had initially though that the white miners' orgy of destruction had engulfed the claim, or that the neighbouring white miners had joined those from town.

Now Ah Wei was saying Lun-Tan's murderers had been looking for him! My Li was distraught; not for the fact that he had narrowly escaped death himself but because innocent Lun-Tan had been killed due to My Li's unwanted connection with the Triad. My Li was speechless. Suffering from shock he sat apart while Simone, Kinqua and Mark picked through the ashes of Lun-Tans' camp to salvage whatever artefacts and implements they could. Some of the neighbouring white miners came over to assist with the clean-up. The others remained protectively watching from their claim.

Like My Li, the miners who came over were under the impression that the demolition of poor Lun-Tan's claim was somehow connected with the racial unrest. Ah Wei and Lun-Tan's assailants had fled at the neighbouring white miners' approach and, in the dark and confusion, they had not realised the perpetrators had been solely Chinese. Among the miners who helped was the man My Li had seen reading the newspaper with the racist cartoon.

'I am sorry this has happened to you,' said the miner. 'We have lived side by side and we know we are all the same colour under our skins. The whites who did this to you are wrong to think the way they do and, although I know it won't bring back your brother,' the man said to Ah Wei, 'I would like to apologise on behalf of my race.'

Ah Wei accepted the white man's extended hand but his agonised eyes were directed at My Li. Ah Wei said nothing to dispel the man's wrong impression of the previous evening's events. Many of the utensils and tools could be rehandled and used and the neighbouring white miners offered to loan Ah Wei their spare tent.

When they had returned to their claim, Ah Wei sought out My Li.

'When Lun-Tan's heart stopped, so mine broke. I bear you no malice My Li but I feel you must leave or further trouble will follow you.'

Gazing at the white men returning to their own claim, Ah Wei added, 'Who knows, perhaps some good will come out of this terrible affair after all.'

My Li collected his few possessions. He looked up to see Kinqua doing the same.

'It is me they want Kinqua. There is no reason for you to leave. Stay here with Ah Wei.'

Kinqua replied, 'I have nothing to keep me here My Li. Your path is my path. We will walk it together.'

And Mark the midshipman said, 'I can't stay around here. If I run into that bunch of thugs I rescued you from, you will have to scrape me off the ground. I would like to come with you too.'

Simone said, 'There is no point in my remaining around here. If my mother and father find me I'll be back in the dwarf's saloon. The best thing I can look forward to is a beating…'

Ah Wei looked at them and said, 'Take the pony cart. Take whatever food, water and gear you may need.' Ah Wei bowed respectfully to My Li. 'If you resolve your trouble with the Triad, I would be happy to greet you again. But until then, stay away. Your karma is heavy for one so young, My Li.'

Before they left, they dug a grave for Lun-Tan and helped Ah Wei put white pennants on poles around the camp. My Li contributed most of what he had earned while working the claim into Lun-Tan's pockets. Kinqua gave his to Ah Wei.

'Your brother will not go hungry on his journey,' My Li said to Ah Wei.

'May you find food for your body and soul for your journey too,' responded Ah Wei.

The sun was already high in the sky as My Li took Lun-Tan's docile pony by its bridle and led it out of the camp' but storm clouds were gathering. Simone and Kinqua rode aboard the pony trap while, over their heads, heavy cumulus clouds tiered layer upon layer up into the stratosphere, brilliantly white where the sunshine played on their upper peripheries, black and foreboding at their base. With the Mark bringing up the rear, walking behind the cart, his belaying pin and the pistol he had commandeered in his belt, they proceeded towards the oncoming storm.

Thunder rumbled intimidatingly and the upper atmosphere was alive with movement and turmoil. At ground level the air was oppressive and still. The white funeral pennants signifying the start of Lun-Tan's journey to the afterlife hung listlessly against their poles. The first huge drops of rain spattered into the dust.

'Where are we heading My Li?' asked Mark.

'We have a friend out there somewhere,' replied My Li.

'Whereabouts?'

'I do not know. But I am going to try and find him. Perhaps he will find us. Baracoona has the ring and whoever has the ring will suffer the fate intended for me. I must regain the ring and return it to the Triad before someone else is hurt.'

'They will kill you anyway.'

'Perhaps. But maybe their vindictiveness will be lessened or forgotten in their delight if they have their ring returned. Perhaps they will slay only me and leave those known to be near to me unharmed.'

'Perhaps… I wouldn't wager on the outcome My Li,' replied Mark.

CHAPTER TWENTY-FOUR

The dwarf puffed out his chest and drew himself up to the limit of his short height. He was standing amid the still smoking rubble of beams and corrugated iron which was all that remained of his fan-tan saloon and house of ill repute.

The Red Poles, Lau and some of his other men were close at hand. All were awed by the devastation of the Chinese quarter. Many shops had been gutted. Those that were not had their windows broken and their advertising hoardings torn down – all had been looted.

'You thought you were so clever,' he sneered at the Red Poles. 'You thought you had them like meat on a plate but all the while you were out there tearing their claim apart, the widow's son was here on our own doorstep!'

'With all respect, Master,' opined Lau. 'It was not our fault. We did not know the widow's son would come snooping into town. We must have missed him by only minutes on the track.'

'Whether you missed him by minutes or hours you still missed him,' retorted the dwarf. He turned to his minions. 'And what were you all doing while the widow's son was wandering around our premises? Where were all of you when the white barbarians were burning down the building.

I could not find one of you! I pay you to protect our assets, of which I am the most important but, when you were needed like never before, you were nowhere to be found. Cowards! You are all cowards. I have hired cowards!'

The Red Poles, Chang and Yung, shifted their feet uncomfortably. Yung was about to say something in reply when one of the dwarf's men came running up to report. The man threw himself to his knees. Out of breath, he had to struggle to complete his sentences between heaves of his overworked lungs.

'You were correct Master. I went to the Lun-Tan claim as you told me to. They were all there – Lun-Tan's brother, Ah Wei, the widow's son, a white man I did not know and the new comfort girl...'

'The new comfort girl too!' the dwarf sarcastically repeated for the benefit of all of those present. 'So, not only does the widow's son steal the seal of the Triad with impunity, he now takes one of our whores as well!'

'There is more Master. The man we questioned at the claim last night is dead. They were making preparations for his burial.'

'How I wish I had someone as clever as this the widow's son working for us!' the dwarf said sardonically. 'These much vaunted Red Poles the White Fan has sent us cannot even kill the right man! They have proved themselves useless and fit only for cleaning water-closets.'

Both Red Poles stiffened and Chang might have forgotten his position if Yung had not gripped his arm.

'Well? What other good news have you brought us?'

'Apart from Ah Wei,' said the man, now in control of his breathing, 'they all left near noon with a pony trap loaded with water and supplies.'

'Excellent,' said the dwarf. 'They've gone to make a nuisance of themselves elsewhere. I am pleased that at least one of my locally trained men can be relied on to carry out his assignment.'

Lau hung his head shamefully.

'At least we will not have to return to the claim as we feared,' Yung said to Chang.

'We wouldn't have had a hope of surprising them a second time. Especially since you unnecessarily killed the older man. He had told us everything he knew. You didn't have to …'

'Argue on your own time please,' cut in the dwarf. 'What other information have you brought us?'

'The white man with them is armed with a pistol.'

'I told you so!' Yung said to Chang. 'Because of you they have armed themselves. This will make it more difficult for us.'

'Keep your squabbles to yourselves,' admonished the dwarf. 'Which way did they go?' he asked his snooper.

'North and west, Master. The cart leaves wheel ruts that will be easy to follow.'

'For some! For some,' said the dwarf.

'Well!' Eyebrows arched expectantly, the dwarf was staring at the Red Poles, 'Well? Aren't you going to request provisions to enable you to pursue them?'

Yung could feel Chang bristling and he ungraciously responded, 'As the White Fan has already instructed you to give us all possible assistance, we thought such a request too obvious to require our asking.'

The dwarf stared at them disdain. 'How many of my men will you require?'

'Two of your men familiar with firearms will be more than sufficient.'

'You hope,' said the dwarf, and he swivelled to face Lau. 'And to please me, you will accompany the brave Red Poles and share their deprivations. You have had too much lazy town living for far too long.'

Dismayed, Lau indicated the ruins of the saloon. 'But what about this?' he asked nasally through his broken nose.

'What are you standing there for?' the dwarf inquired of his other dumbfounded minions. 'Rebuild it!'

The dwarf turned his back on Lau and the Red Poles and strutted off to his temporary offices in the loft above a nearby produce provender's warehouse. It was full of baled hay and the dust made him constantly sneeze.

Over at the Christian Church, the corpses of those killed during the previous night's rioting, both yellow and white, were being laid out in front of the altar.

One of the white cadavers was Simone's father. The blacksmith had been one of the loudest, most vociferous voices at the assembly in front of the church, where the prelude to the rioting took place.

When the enraged mob swarmed up the main street to the joss-house, the blacksmith had advanced with them. Not only did he consider their descent to lynch law an opportunity to enjoy himself with some punching, clouting, kicking and pummelling, but also as a chance to indulge in some open thieving that would be acceptable if someone saw him in the act. When the mob reached the Chinese temple, someone yelled: 'They use the joss-house for safe-keeping! Look out for hidden treasure!'

While many of the rioters simply vented their spleen in the orgy of destruction, the blacksmith and other reprobates of like mind searched for valuables and secret caches. The furnishings were already well ablaze when he found a slab in the floor without mortar to hold it in place. With the help of another man and the aid of a curtain rod, they managed to lever up the slab.

His helper looked up, and started, cried: 'Leave it! The roof is alight! We can come back afterwards!'

'Hang on! We'll have it clear in a jiffy!'

'No way! I'm getting out of here.'

The blacksmith could see something glinting, like gold, in the light of the flames. When his helper fled outside, the blacksmith stayed, his greed greater than his instinct for self-preservation.

Ignoring the heat, something he was familiar with from his hours at the forge, the blacksmith threw back the heavy slab and, with his free hand, he reached into the cavity. It was an ancient bronze ceremonial urn, imported from China with care and reverence, and extremely valuable, but not to the blacksmith. As he hurled it aside in disgust, the ceiling and its beams crashed down upon him. His charred body was recovered at first light and taken to the church.

Above the church steeple, the same storm that had enveloped My Li, Kinqua, Mark and Simone grumbled its warning of approaching bad weather; its billowing blanket of foreboding clouds shutting out the sun. A flash of lightning stabbed through the gloom and desultory drops of rain hit and hissed as they struck the still glowing beams of the burnt out buildings. By the time the Red Poles and their men were ready to set out, the sporadic drops had turned into a steady downpour accompanied by violent gusts of wind.

Already soaked to their skins, My Li, Kinqua, Mark and Simone had not sought shelter from the storm. Determined to put as much distance as they could between themselves and Ah Wei – so that no further misfortune might befall him – My Li and his companions marched headlong into the fury of the tempest. The pouring rain streaked and washed the layers of make-up from Simone's face. Kinqua draped a groundsheet around his and Simone's shoulders as protection from the deluge that fell with such force it smarted on impact. Mark slung his seafarer's jacket over his shoulders and tried to prevent his revolver getting wet. My Li made no attempt to protect himself from the driving rain and gave his friends the impression he was oblivious to the ferocity of the elements raging around them.

Deeply preoccupied with his own thoughts and, since leaving Ah Wei, pursued not only by the Red Poles but by the demons of self-pity and pessimism, My Li was obsessively recalling Lun-Tan's tale of the Flying Dutchman, which he had told them about during the cheerful evenings they shared. He wondered whether it was his destiny to bring disaster to those he cared for like the accursed Dutchman?

But, by ignoring the storm and making the most of the hours available to them for travelling, My Li and his companions thwarted the Red Poles' opportunity to catch up with their quarry that day. For the torrential rain caused dormant creeks to resume their flow; the resultant runoff caused erosion and subsidence's in the gullies and, in the diggings, shafts flooded or collapsed under the saturated weight of the soil. The rain also washed away any trace of the ruts left by the wheels of the trap, the imprints of the pony's hooves and the fugitives' footsteps.

When My Li, Kinqua, Mark and Simone stopped at nightfall and took shelter in a derelict, bark-roofed shepherd's hut to try to prepare a hot meal and dry out their sodden clothing, the Red Poles and the three men allocated to them by the dwarf were several kilometres away, searching an area that had turned to swamp underfoot. After covering the leaks in the roof with a groundsheet and placing stones on it to prevent it disappearing into the inky darkness, the pursued lit a fire and, after warming themselves, dried clothes, blankets and cooked.

By the time they were settling down to a comparatively comfortable night's rest, their tired and infuriated pursuers had come to realise they were not going to capture their prey that night.

The instant conclusion to their task [insert 'which']the Red Poles were seeking had eluded them. Their men were soaked, hungry and complaining. The Red Poles had expected to be back in town by nightfall and had not made preparations for a prolonged search. Momentarily defeated, they returned to town to collect provisions, and to suffer the dwarf's derision in silence.

'How long will you need my men for?' gibed the dwarf. 'Three months? Six months? You haven't got that long before you become wanted men yourselves?'

'Six weeks,' replied Yung. 'If we haven't found the widow's son by then, the men can return to you, for we, or the widow's son will be dead.'

'You shall have your men and supplies,' said dwarf. 'The White Fan will not be informed that I failed to assist you…'

The following morning was grey and dismal but the rain had diminished in intensity to drizzle with occasional heavy falls. The Red Poles, re-equipped for a lengthy period in the bush, renewed their hunt. For five days of intermittent rain they found nothing to indicate My Li's presence or whereabouts. On the morning of the sixth, they came across muddy wheel ruts weaving between decaying logs and broken ground. Their route led north-west. Their find was confirmed by a market gardener taking manure to his vegetables. 'That's right! Three men and a woman. Friends of yours you say. Well, if you ask me, you'll be lucky to catch up to them. They've got a good start on you!'

'We did not ask you,' Chang had retorted.

Three days after the Red Poles and their party found the ruts left by the passing of the pony cart, Baracoona was jogging over the same landscape at a distance devouring lope when he bisected the ruts.

For months Baracoona had remained in the district waiting for the Red Poles to leave the vicinity of the town. Always lighting his fire in a position where he could observe the main road to and from the diggings, Baracoona systematically examined any footprints he found. Usually, little more than a cursory glance revealed that the footprint or sign held no meaning for him. He had pored over thousands of prints. But this time, when Baracoona reached the ruts left by the pony trap, he froze, his features immobile, his eyes alert and interested. Baracoona crouched; his hand reached out to gently caress the indentation left by a foot that bore more weight to its outer side.

Baracoona had seen the footprint before – all the way from Heaven's Gate to Lambing Flat. He also recognised the footprints of someone who was special to him – the man who had saved his life – My Li, the Yellow Man, and those belonging to his white-bearded friend. Baracoona grimaced and then glanced at the sinking sun as if measuring how much time he had before the sun sank altogether and stopped him from following the Red Poles' tracks. Then he turned in the direction the footsteps led and resumed his kilometre consuming run. Around his neck hung the ring – the seal of the Triad, given to him by My Li. It glowed redly in the light of the setting sun.

CHAPTER TWENTY-FIVE

The rain became relegated to memory. It would be the last rain they saw for some time. At first, the countryside was lush from its recent drenching and rich with wildlife. Streams ran freely and every gully yielded a pool of muddy runoff water which the pony and its passengers drank with relish whenever they were thirsty. Every day – and sometimes into the cool of the night – they walked towards the north-east, in the direction My Li remembered Baracoona pointing to his homeland. But the weeks went by without contact with Baracoona.

As they travelled, the country they crossed became more and more desolate, but its true nature was disguised by the plentiful amount of surface water. Although they did not know it, they were entering one of the world's most inhospitable deserts, momentarily green from the recent moisture. Tiny plants that had waited years to bloom had flowered with the coming of the rain.

Now the pools were evaporating and damp patches of mud appeared where water had so recently collected. The mud dried, fissured and flaked in rind-like wafers; then crumbled and returned to dust. The animal life that had been abundant when they set out became scarcer.

193

Earlier in their trek, Mark the midshipman managed, at the expense of only one cartridge, to bring down a plump wallaby, which they roasted. Three weeks later he had repeated the exploit but used up two bullets in the process. As only three bullets remained in the revolver, they were cautious about using the last of their ammunition, believing it to be more prudent to retain the few remaining cartridges in case of an emergency. The supplies they had packed into the trap when they left were almost gone.

Six weeks had elapsed since My Li, Kinqua, Simone and Mark had left Ah Wei grieving for his brother at the claim by the river. Over forty days of wandering in the wilderness, the sun showed them no pity. It beat down with relentless rays upon the now dry earth and the travellers trudging across its surface. Not a cloud was in sight to offer them shade and relief. The ground was hard again and cracked like oven-baked bread in an oven. Trees were few and far between. Their branches and leaves drooped under the onslaught of the sun. Where there was grass, it was already dry, brown and shrivelling. Where there were boulders, they were too hot to touch. The heat radiated off the ground in shimmering waves that played tricks upon the eye and made water-like mirages ripple and pool in the distance. Whenever they stood still, it was like standing on hot coals. The breathless air felt ready to ignite and surface water was becoming difficult to find. For three days they had walked around the edge of a salt-pan that reflected light like a mirror, so brightly it was painful to their eyes and made them involuntarily weep.

To rest their failing feet, they took turns at riding for an hour at a time on the trap pulled without complaint by Lun-Tan's stalwart animal. Whoever was happily being jostled from side to side as the trap lurched beneath them was regarded with envy by the others, walking footsore and perspiring behind it.

But now the trap was tilted on its side and Kinqua was soothing the frightened pony and releasing it from its harness. My Li, Mark and Simone were examining the wheel that had dropped into a crack and become wedged between some rocks. 'The rim is shattered and the metal binding band was sprung away...'

'There are broken spokes too ...'

'This cart won't be going any further ...' Mark said and he wiped his brow with the back of his hand.

Mark's white officer's shirt, its starched wing-collar undone, but still attached, was open to his midriff and wet with sweat. Where his body was exposed, rivulets of perspiration trickled through the dust that coated his body.

My Li had to swallow twice to bring spittle to his mouth. 'Give the pony a drink and release it. It is unfair for the animal to perish because of us. It will find its way back.'

'Back? Back where?' Mark turned through three hundred and sixty degrees. The horizon was flat in every direction. Not a hill nor any other kind of landmark could be seen. My Li shrugged his shoulders.

'Do you have any idea where we are My Li?'

My Li shook his head.

'We could die of thirst out here My Li. Your Triad acquaintances will catch up and will only have to bury us!'

'I am hoping Baracoona will find us first. There is nothing to keep you here if you don't want to be.'

'In for a penny, in for a pound,' replied the Mark. 'Besides, it is a long way anywhere from here.'

'What now?' asked Simone, staring at the broken wheel.

'We take what we can carry and walk on.'

The difference in having to tramp all day without the hour or two of rest on the pony trap was considerable.

As the sun dropped to the western horizon and suffused the sky with a crimson glow, they were all staggering from exhaustion.

Kinqua suffered most from the debilitating effects of dehydration. My Li who walked with him, giving him support when he required it and talking and laughing with him when the old man was able to proceed on his own.

When Mark tore off the grubby remnant of his shirt's wing-collar, throwing it on the ground and cursing his stupidity in accompanying them, it was My Li who goaded him with the accusation that white men had no endurance. He baited him to prove his mettle until Mark became so angry he began to laugh, a laugh that conveyed more than a small note of hysteria. To Simone, My Li was kind and helpful, buoying her will to continue.

'Troubles are like the accumulation of storm clouds. After a lot of noise and discomfort the skies soon clear.'

'You're beginning to sound more like Kinqua every day,' Simone's laughter was weak with tiredness.

Four more days on foot and they were reaching the end of their tether. Their eyes were sore and rheumy from the constant glare, their throats parched and their lips cracked from having to eke out the meagre rations of water they were carrying with them. My Li saw Kinqua was tottering. 'Would you like to rest, Kinqua?'

Kinqua shook his head grimly. 'Walk on,' he croaked.

'What's that?' grunted Mark.

On a cluster of boulders before them was the slender silhouette of an Aboriginal. He was leaning on his spear with his left foot resting on his right knee, as My Li had often seen Baracoona stand. My Li thought that he had found whom he was seeking, and broke into a shambling run towards the aboriginal.

'Baracoona!' he cried hoarsely. 'Baracoona!'

The Aboriginal lowered his leg and tightened his grip on his spear. Whereas My Li, Kinqua, Mark and Simone were struggling to cope with the harsh environment in which they found themselves, the Aboriginal showed no discomfort at all. But he did appear disturbed by their distraught condition. My Li stopped short of the Aboriginal and caught his breath. The man was bearded and was not Baracoona.

'Baracoona?' asked My Li. 'Where is Baracoona?'

The Aboriginal smiled and nodded his head emphatically. My Li, more desperately, tried again. 'Baracoona? Where can we find him?' But the Aboriginal merely clapped his hands and nodded happily again.

My Li remembered the tjurunga, and he fumbled open the apothecary satchel he still carried. He drew out the tjurunga Baracoona had given him and held it up for the Aboriginal to see. The Aboriginal's attitude changed immediately. 'Baracoona,' repeated My Li.

The Aboriginal sombrely pointed in the direction of the sunset, the direction in which they were headed, and stared at My Li in awe. My Li recalled the word Baracoona used for water. 'Ngama,' he requested. 'Water …'

The Aboriginal leapt down from his rock and strode to the northern side of the group of boulders he had been standing on.

Bending between the small boulders, the Aboriginal picked up some dead vegetation to reveal a deep bottle-necked hole in the rock. It was full to the brim with clear potable water.

'Oh God!' said Mark and fell to his knees in grateful thanks. One by one they drank from the water in the rock and the aboriginal applauded each of them as they did so. When they had slaked their thirst, the Aboriginal covered the water in the rock with the vegetation again to prevent evaporation.

My Li gazed at the boulders and at the sinking sun.

'There is shelter here for the night. Why don't we rest here and go in the direction the Aborigine indicated in the morning. From his reaction, he must know or have heard of Baracoona. We are close to him. I am sure of it!'

When My Li turned back to the Aboriginal, the man was no longer there.

As that same day's sun set behind the boulders against which My Li and his companions were resting, a wedge-tailed eagle flew high over the barren terrain in search of prey, stalking lizards and mammals emerging from the burrows where they had hidden from the heat of day. The eagle wheeled and soared on the convection currents of heated air rising from the plain. Below it, My Li's, Kinqua's, Mark's and Simone's footsteps stretched to the darkening eastern horizon.

The eagle swooped lower, its eyes fixed on the scuff marks and scraped earth where the passing feet had dislodged stones and overturned pebbles. A small lizard had been disturbed from its cranny. The eagle descended, but as it plummeted ground-wards it spied five men squatting, sitting, lying beside the path taken by My Li, Kinqua, Mark and Simone, and with an instant course correction, it swerved and effortlessly soared back into the sky.

Unperturbed by the eagle's presence, the men, with the Red Poles leading them and their stomachs full of cooked pony meat, rose and continued towards the sunset. The Red Poles were aware that the four sets of footprints they were following had hardly deviated in a week of walking. However, they did not know how far ahead of them their quarry might be – or that they had narrowed My Li's lead to two or three hours. The Red Poles decided to decrease whatever the gap was between the parties by pushing on blindly for a few extra hours after nightfall. They knew there was a risk – more likely the probability – of losing the tracks they were pursuing in the dark, but believed they would easily find them again after a quick scout around the next morning. The Red Poles considered the odds were in their favour and that, by doing so, they might hasten the final resolution of their task.

The first night watch was Mark the midshipman's.

While the others slept close to the soak revealed to them by the Aboriginal, Mark sat apart in a cleft in the rocks. But being on watch in the middle of the Australian desert was totally different to that at sea. There was no deck swaying under his feet; no sudden yaw or dip into a wave compelling him to grab the nearest handrail to prevent himself falling overboard and shaking him out of his fatigue; no salt-spray across his face or cut of wind to tousle his hair – only a smooth rock to brace his back against and silence that was loud to the ears. For an hour Mark managed to keep awake, snapping his head upright whenever he found his chin touching his chest. Then his head sank slowly forward, and Mark fell soundly asleep.

Mark woke knowing something was wrong. He lifted his head and listened. An insect chirped among the rocks. The stars were suspended like a low solid mass above him. Not even a breath of wind sighed over the land. Then he heard the crunch of a footstep on the sand and stones.

Through the cleft in the rock he could see the cotton garbed legs and slippers that could only belong to a Chinese. Could it be My Li or Kinqua thought Mark? Impossible; My Li wore boots and Kinqua sandals he recollected. The bottom half of the man's body he could see between the rocks was approached by another. More feet grated against the ground and Mark could hear the low murmur of strangers' voices.

There was no doubt about it. The voices were speaking in Chinese but Mark did not recognise them as belonging to either My Li or Kinqua.

He could differentiate at least four or five separate voices. They could only be the Triad members My Li feared were sworn to kill him – and most likely anyone else with My Li when they caught up with him.

Every natural instinct cried out to Mark to call a warning, but logic and his sailing experience – that taught him to remain cool in a crisis – restrained him.

From what he could see in the starlight, not only were they outnumbered but also caught unawares because of his dereliction of duty.

A stab of anguish brought Mark to the realisation they had only one chance to elude discovery. Providing My Li, Kinqua and Simone remained sound asleep and did not snore or make a noise, there was a possibility the Triad members might move on. They did not know about the soak among the boulders, and must be travelling in the cool of the night in an attempt to catch up with his own party. Haste was their priority. By keeping quiet, their presence among the boulders might be concealed.

More voices exchanged comments in Chinese. Someone lent against the boulder at the outlet from the cleft where Mark sat and, as he slowly dragged himself further back into the rocks and groped for leverage, something slender writhed beneath his hand. An overwhelming sensation of horror ran through him as he withdrew his hand. He was sharing the cleft in the rocks with a snake.

Mark had no way of knowing whether the reptile was venomous or not and he reached for the pistol he had placed on the ground beside him when he had earlier made himself comfortable. There were still three rounds in the chambers but, as he peered into the dark, he knew it was futile. Although he could feel the snake's presence he could not see it. If he blindly fired the revolver the Chinese would be alerted and he, My Li, Kinqua and Simone would, even with a fight, die at their ruthless hands. Mark lowered the pistol and, to prevent himself crying out aloud, gritted his teeth as he felt the snake sink in its fangs – once, and then twice – into the flesh of his forearm.

CHAPTER TWENTY-SIX

My Li woke beside the soak-hole. He felt rested and refreshed – too refreshed. The stars were faint in the sky. The dawn of a new day was competing with them for brightness, and the stars were fading fast. My Li was meant to have taken the middle night watch, as Mark nautically referred to it; the midnight to pre-dawn watch. But Mark had not shaken him awake as they had agreed. My Li sat up and stretched to straighten out the kinks and stiffness that had crept into his bones while sleeping on the ground. Kinqua and Simone were still sleeping and, without disturbing them, My Li rose and went to find Mark.

Mark had not moved from his position. His eyes were open and fixed on something that had caught his attention in the far distance. As My Li moved towards him, Mark's gaze did not waver. Nor did his eyes switch their focus to My Li's approach.

My Li eased himself into the cramped space in the cleft in the rocks. He touched Mark's cheek with the back of his hand and found the midshipman's skin already cold.

My Li manoeuvred himself into a position where he could grip Mark's body under the armpits and managed to drag his corpse, already stiffening with rigour mortis, out of the cleft of the rock.

The snake had long gone and My Li was unable to comprehend what had occurred for some time. Then he noticed the two sets of puncture wounds on Mark's forearm. Leaving the midshipman in the shade of the boulders, My Li climbed on top of one of the boulders and surveyed the surrounding desert.

The landscape was stony with patches of sand, scattered bushes and the occasional clump of stunted trees. Where there was sand, it had been blown into long, low dunes by the wind that swept without obstruction over the vast expanse of the empty plain. In the early morning light, with the sun above the horizon, the shallow angle of its beams created an illusion of waves instead of sand dunes. From where My Li was standing, the dunes resembled an undulating ocean and he again recalled Lun-Tan's tale of the doomed Dutchman. In his mind's eye, a small cloud on the horizon became a ship. My Li heard flapping above his head and, although when he looked up he saw the noise was caused by the wings of an eagle hovering high above his head, the sound reminded him of the slapping of canvas against the mainyard and masts of a ship at sea. The cream coloured and fluffy clouds overhead took on the characteristic shapes of sails bent before the breeze. Overwhelmed with sorrow but not knowing the true extent of Mark's sacrifice, My Li climbed down from the boulders and went to wake Kinqua and Simone.

Unable to dig deeply without the proper tools, they scratched at the ground with their knives and the twisted sticks they found under the scattered, gnarled bushes, until they had scooped out a shallow grave. My Li and Kinqua laid Mark into his final resting place.

Simone found a weathered stone which she put under Mark's head as a pillow.

Before they pushed the dirt back over Mark's body, Simone covered his face with a handkerchief she had carried in her pocket. The dirt barely covered Mark's corpse, so they collected rocks and gently placed them, one by one, over his body until they had constructed a cairn almost a metre high. As a token of Mark's Christian faith, Kinqua made a cross from two twigs and inserted it in a crack between rocks at the head of the cairn.

My Li, Kinqua and Simone looked at each other. Simone's eyes were tearful but bright and full of faith and trust in her companions. Kinqua's eyes reflected the sadness he felt for Mark's passing but twinkled with intelligence and determination. My Li's eyes were sunk in dark ringed sockets and empty of any expression.

'What do we do now?' Simone asked her Chinese friends. Kinqua appeared to be waiting for My Li to answer but the younger man said nothing. My Li stared blankly at the cairn.

'What do we do?' Kinqua finally repeated Simone's question. 'We do the only thing we can do. We walk on.' Picking up his water-bag and the few possessions he had tied in a blanket when they left the pony trap behind, he took Simone's arm and steered her away from the grave. Simone and Kinqua covered a hundred metres or more before My Li finally tore himself away from the cairn and, putting Mark's pistol into his apothecary's bag, followed them into the desert.

They walked without speaking.

A few hours later the bearded Aboriginal appeared out of a fold in the ground and rattled his spears against his small wooden shield – used to deflect missiles thrown at him. Kinqua, Simone and My Li stopped but the Aboriginal shook his spear again and, shouting something they did not comprehend, thrust their barbed points in a direction to their left. 'I think he wants us to go more that way instead of the way we are going,' said Simone.

'I will ask him,' said Kinqua. And he ambled over towards the Aboriginal.

But the warrior strode further away from him, gesturing fiercely at Kinqua to go in the direction he was pointing. Kinqua waited while Simone and My Li caught up to him. 'I think we should do as he wishes.'

They changed course, veering on to the bearing the warrior indicated. The Aboriginal seemed pleased. He nodded his head in approval and called out to them in his own language, which they did not understand. They walked on and once the Aboriginal was satisfied they had reconciled themselves to the change in direction he had advocated, the warrior disappeared into the folds and hummocks in the red earth, imperceptible from a distance.

It was past mid-afternoon when, after shuffling at a tired snail's pace up a slight incline, they topped a ridge. In doing so, a sight was revealed to them that, because of its majesty and breathtaking beauty, its memory would stay with them for the remainder of their lives.

There before them lay another panorama of empty plain, extending as far as their eyes could see in every direction. But, in the middle distance was a single, huge hill of red rock, towering above the flatness and, by its height dominating and making the plain appear even more level than it was. The red rock was scored with crevices and cremations [change to 'crenations']. The shadows of swiftly moving clouds passing over it caused the rock to vary and fluctuate in colour and hue, as if it was an animate being. Because it was such an awesome object in the middle of nowhere, the rock gave My Li, Simone and Kinqua the impression that the rest of the world radiated out from it – that they had reached the centre of the earth.

Shafts of sunlight shone between the scudding clouds. One moment the rock lay in shadow and the next it was bathed in the bright light of day. Neither one or the other dominated for very long before either sunlight or shade replaced it. The onlookers imagined a warlike struggle between light and dark was in progress before their eyes. Kinqua spoke first.

'...where the thorny devils guard the red rock that holds the sky above the earth,' he said huskily, recalling Baracoona's words. And the rock did indeed appear as if it was a pillar holding up the sky above the earth.

My Li looked at Kinqua. The old man's face was ashen. 'What is wrong Kinqua, you look like someone has stepped on your grave?'

'Whoever it was has a heavy tread,' replied Kinqua.

'But what of the thorny devils? What did he mean by that?'

Simone had the answer. She pointed to the ground in front of them. Barring their way to the rock was a lizard. No longer than the length of My Li's foot, its hooded eyes glared aggressively at the intruders into its territory. The lizard opened and shut its mouth and held its ground at their approach. It had a leathery skin with a line of thorny spikes down its spine to the tip of its tail. Other horny spikes stuck out of its legs, skull and flanks.

Simone's saddened eyes sparkled at the sight of the ridiculous little lizard that was prepared to confront the much larger creatures that had entered its realm. The lizard refused to move from their path until they were almost on top of it – then it gave in and retreated on ungainly, waddling legs, bounding out of their path.

Simone indicated another lizard skulking under a rock. Kinqua almost stood on another, its mottled skin blending into its environment so well that it was perfectly camouflaged until it broke cover to escape his foot.

'This is the sacred place Baracoona spoke of,' said Kinqua. 'I can feel it.'

They approached the mountainous rock that reared out of the earth. 'It is like the peak of a buried mountain,' said My Li, almost forgetting how the day had begun in his astonishment at finding such an incredible solitary landmark in the midst of the antipodean emptiness.

Kinqua led the way, walking with a spring to his step that My Li had never seen before. His years and his tiredness seemed to drop away from him.

For the first time since they had met, My Li imagined what Kinqua must have been like as a young man – sprightly, inquisitive, athletic – and never lacking in humour. As they came closer, Kinqua held out his arms towards the rock like someone warming their hands before a fire. Even Kinqua's slender fingers were extended towards it. My Li had once seen a water-diviner searching for subterranean sources of water for a well behave similarly when he was a youngster in his village in China. But My Li knew Kinqua wasn't feeling the whereabouts of water. Kinqua turned to My Li. His face was radiant.

'Now I know why our paths were ordained to cross – why it was you walked into my room in Canton!'

The great mass of the monolith towered over them. The ground around the base of the rock was, in places, covered with detritus that had broken away from its sides and fallen. In other places green grasses grew where run-off provided nutrient. Big boulders and fissures in the rock showed where, greater, geographical forces had been at work, peeling the rock away in onion like layers and cracking it with mighty tectonic pressures.

As the three reached the bottom of the rock, at a site where breakaway boulders were haphazardly piled however they had come to rest after falling from the cliff face above – a man stepped into sight from behind the rubble. This time it was not an Aboriginal. He was Chinese. Another Chinese appeared from behind the boulders. The two Chinese were less than ten metres away and My Li knew that, one way or another, he too had reached the end of his journey. For even from that distance he could see the scar that deformed the bigger man's nose where it met his lip.

Neither Simone nor Kinqua needed My Li to tell them who the newcomers were or what they represented. The three of them stopped in mid-stride. Kinqua looked to their left for a way of withdrawing and Simone to the right and rear. Behind them, from where they had been screened by rocks and scrubby bushes, emerged the three Triad men sent by the dwarf to assist the Red poles in their search for My Li.

'What kept you?' jeered Chang, the Red Pole with the mutilated nose.

My Li could only stare at him.

CHAPTER TWENTY-SEVEN

Escape was impossible. Two of the dwarf's men accompanying the Red poles were armed with pistols and the third, the man known as Lau, with a single action rifle. My Li found himself looking into the contemptuous and mocking eyes of the big man with the disfigured nose. This was the Triad executioner who needed no second bidding to murder Tiao; who did not even blink as her blood gushed and sprayed from her headless torso as it tottered and walked a pace before falling like a felled tree in the forest; the killer who considered Tiao's head in the gutter to be fair work for his pay.

My Li knew these were the Red Poles who had pursued him half-way across the world. The same two men he had first seen on the road outside his village, while he hid, terrified, in the drainage ditch, so long ago in China. My Li knew that he could not expect mercy from the Red pole named Chang.

Chang wore his disfigurement as if it was a badge of office; as if the pain he had once endured gave him a permit to inflict suffering to others.

'Allow us to introduce ourselves' said Chang, and he bowed with superciliously insolent formality. 'My name is Chang and my associate's name is Yung.'

Chang did not bother to introduce the dwarf's men. 'We are soldiers of the Black Scarf Triad and, in the name of our Five Ancestors, we have been sent to this barbarous and barren country to retrieve something you, the Widow Song Li's Son, stole from our illustrious society…'

'I know who you are,' interrupted My Li. 'And don't bother to give yourself airs and graces and attempt to justify your criminal activities with titles and noble sounding traditions. For you are nothing more than a murderer. The murderer I saw slay my sister and, most likely, the same murderer who slew the worthy miner Lun-Tan. I suspect you are also responsible for the deaths of a dozen innocent aboriginals at the gorge known as Heaven's Gate, and that all these killings I know about are only a fraction of your ugly activities. I think I also know what you are after …'

'The ring,' sighed Chang and held out his hand and waited for My Li to place it in his palm. 'The ring if you please. Our masters would like it returned.'

'So you were right, Kinqua,' said My Li. 'They were after the ring I picked up on the night Tiao was killed.'

'The ring!' insisted Chang.

'Why is the ring so important that you should spend over a year of your lives to get it back?' asked Kinqua.

Chang slowly lowered his hand. 'The ring you stole is the seal of the Triad. Our masters are extremely angry…'

'A seal!' exclaimed Kinqua, suddenly comprehending why the youth he had befriended had been so persistently pursued. 'No wonder they sent you this far!'

'And now they want it back …' Chang held out his hand again.

'I don't have the ring,' admitted My Li.

Yung spoke for the first time:

'Perhaps I should tell you we are instructed to punish the thief who stole the seal. But if you hand it over to us without further fuss or bother, we will forget that part of our orders and leave you all here, alive…'

My Li looked at Chang and knew that the man who killed Tiao in cold-blood and who had pursued him across the Southern Sea and the Australian desert would not agree to a compromise that spared their lives. My Li was concerned for Kinqua and Simone's lives as well as his own. If he simply told the Red Poles he had thought the ring to be a worthless bauble and had given it to an Aboriginal in a symbolic exchange to express his friendship, these hard-hearted men would see their captives as useless and expendable, and slit their throats before going in search of Baracoona. My Li decided his and his friends' one slim chance of survival, was to make the Red Poles believe he actually had the ring or knew where it was – otherwise they were dead.

'I would be stupid to simply hand the ring over to you. What is in it for me if I give it to you?'

'As I said, make it easy for us and we will spare your lives,' offered Yung.

'…and if I don't have the ring,' asked My Li.

Chang bent and picked up My Li's apothecary satchel. With one irate yank, Chang ripped open the bag and tipped My Li's meticulously labelled ointments, herbs, medicines and Mark's pistol, which My Li had salvaged, onto the ground.

Chang removed the remaining bullets and tossed the pistol aside. He crouched and broke open every jar and bottle to ensure the missing ring had not been concealed inside an unguent. On not finding the ring, he tore the interior lining from the bag and shook it like someone removing crumbs from a table-cloth. He then went through Simone and Kinqua's meagre possessions – all to no avail.

Becoming angrier, exasperated at being so near and yet so far from success and their own salvation, Chang brusquely ordered Lau, 'Search them!'

'I'll search the girl!' One of the local recruits armed with a pistol offered slyly. He was an uncouth looking character with a goatee beard on the point of his chin.

My Li's heart sank as he realised the grave situation in which he had involved Kinqua and Simone, the two people he cared most about in the world. My Li decided there was nothing to be gained by stalling.

He decided to change tack and tell the Red Poles the truth. 'You won't find it on her. I gave it to an Aboriginal.'

'You gave it to an Aboriginal!' harped Yung. 'You gave the seal of the Black Scarf Triad to a naked savage?'

'Yes,' replied My Li. 'I didn't know the ring might be of importance at the time. I didn't know...'

'You didn't know?' ridiculed Chang. 'You didn't know? You mean to tell us you didn't know what you were doing? You stole the seal of our lodge in retaliation for what happened to your sister! Why else would you sail the southern sea on one of the white Men's hell ships and then lead us on a chase all over this unbearable and barren continent? How dare you try to tell us you did not know what you were doing!'

'It's true,' Kinqua chimed in. 'He, we, had no idea of the value of the ring to your society until after My Li had given it away.'

'We will see about that!' snarled Chang. My Li's earlier attempt to distract the Red Poles by asking what was in it for himself, if he handed over the ring, had sown doubt and Chang's patience was at an end.

'Bind them,' he ordered.

The two Red Poles were apparently in charge, as the other men quickly obeyed Chang's instruction.

With the rifle levelled and cocked in case My Li, Kinqua or Simone foolishly tried to make a vain run for it, the uncouth character with the goatee beard and the other local Triad member securely bound their hands behind their backs.

Chang produced a black silk scarf bearing the ideograph of the Triad screen-printed in white onto one corner. 'Take the girl and the grey-beard to the cave we found and roll the rock across the entrance. Only one of you need stay to guard them. Two of you return here once they are safely inside the cave.'

'And don't touch them!' ordered the Red Pole called Yung. 'We may need to ask them some questions to confirm whatever we learn from the widow's son.'

In the moments before the black scarf blocked out his sight, My Li watched as Kinqua and Simone were herded, stumbling, up the scree slope, difficult with lose stones and unsettled gravel, towards a tuck in the rock face. Then his interrogation began.

My Li was seated blindfolded on a rock not far from where they had inadvertently walked into the arms of his enemies. Chang monotonously asked him the same question. 'Where is the ring?'

My Li's reply was equally repetitive.

'I do not know.'

Nearly every time My Li answered, Chang would strike him viciously about the face, neck, shoulders and body. Being blindfolded, My Li never knew from which direction the next blow would be coming from. Chang quietly walked around him, unleashing his attacks from behind My Li, in front of him or to either side. Unable to prepare himself, every slap or punch took My Li by surprise, therefore increasing the shock effect of the beating.

Although the thuggery had been going on for less than twenty minutes before two of the dwarf's men returned, slithering over the loose stones of the scree slope without Simone or Kinqua, to My Li it felt like an eternity.

'Are they safely in the cave?'

'Yes,' replied Lau.

'Then go over there somewhere until we have finished here.'

'I would like to watch,' said a voice My Li recognised as the yokel with the goatee who had asked to be allowed to search Simone. 'The skill of the Red Poles is renowned.'

'If you please,' said Chang. 'But don't open your mouth or I'll close it for you.'

My Li did not need to see the effect of Chang's blows to know he had become a mass of bruises. His face was stiff and swollen and he was finding it difficult to phrase his responses. His lips were split, some of his teeth were loose and the salt taste of blood was awash in his mouth.

The Red Pole named Chang knew a hundred ways to make My Li feel pain. Having battered My Li's face black and blue, he decided to try a more subtle method of making his victim reveal the whereabouts of the ring. Chang cut a sliver off a stock of wood and inserted it under the nail of the forefinger of My Li's right hand. My Li screamed in agony.

'Now tell us where it is! Tell us and your suffering will cease!' insisted Yung.

'I have told you! I don't know where the ring is. The Aboriginal I gave it to could be anywhere by now!'

'Who was this Aboriginal? Where did you meet him?'

'I met him at Heaven's Gate. He was almost dead from arsenic poisoning. We helped him recover.'

Although My Li could not see them, the Red Poles' eyes narrowed and they exchanged concerned glances.

214

'I thought you said you checked them and they were all dead?' Chang bristled petulantly.

'I did,' affirmed Yung.

'You could not have – or else he is lying.'

'Surely ...' Yung agreeably said to My Li. '...if you exchanged tokens of friendship with this native, he must have told you what he intended to do after you parted?'

My Li did not reply.

Chang struck him across the bridge of his nose. My Li felt his nose begin to bleed.

'Where did you last see him?' demanded Yung. 'Tell us everything you know and this violence will stop. Make it easy for yourself.'

'I last saw him near Lambing Flat, the day we arrived at the diggings ...' My Li told them.

'And the Aboriginal?' queried Chang. 'Where did he go? What did he plan to do?'

'He planned to kill you,' My Li informed Chang.

Chang sniffed his scorn. 'It will take more than a primitive savage to kill a Red Pole.

'Where will we find this Aboriginal?' asked Yung.

'I don't know.'

'I don't know! I don't know!' exploded Chang. 'Is that all you can say? You sound like a trained parrot and I don't believe you! Tell us where to find this Aboriginal. Tell us! Tell us!'

Chang began to hail blows upon My Li's unprotected head. My Li was knocked from his perch on the rock by the force of Chang's punches and he pitched full-length on the ground. Infuriated by what he saw as My Li's refusal to divulge where Baracoona, and therefore the ring, might be found, Chang lashed out with his feet, kicking at My Li's prostrate body.

'Tell us where the ring is! Your life and the lives of your friends aren't the only ones at stake! Tell us! Tell us!'

'Enough!' cried Yung. 'Stop it or you will kill him! He's no use to us dead!'

'He's no use to us alive unless he can be made to reveal the whereabouts of the ring. And if he is telling us the truth about giving it away to this Aboriginal friend of his, then we have little time left to us in which to find him. The widow's son must be made to talk!'

'You fool Chang! You only know one approach, don't you? There are other ways to make him talk besides the use of force …'

'If you are sensitive and the sight of blood offends you, look the other way.'

'Be sensible Chang! If you badly hurt him we will never find the ring.'

'If we don't find the ring we are dead men ourselves. The Widow's Son is our only hope of regaining the ring. I will make him want to tell us where it is. Before I'm finished he will be pleading to be permitted to tell us…'

'But what if he doesn't know…'

'Then his death does not matter…'

Lying on the ground and barely conscious after the punishment he had absorbed, My Li listened to the two Red Poles arguing with incredulity. He could hear Chang's feet scraping the ground within centre metres of his head. Suddenly dirt was sent flying into his blindfolded face and Chang's feet were joined by others. For a second My Li thought the dust and pebbles had been deliberately kicked at him but, as he listened to the grunts and scuffling, he became aware that the Red Poles were fighting each other.

For well over a year the two Red Poles had been searching for My Li. Now, having finally found him, they had discovered the widow Song Li's son either did not have the ring they were sworn to return to China or that he was not prepared to tell them where it was.

For over a year the two men had lived in each other's pockets, sharing trials and tribulations and travelling by sea and land with the pressure of a death sentence if they failed to complete their task within the allotted time.

Having finally caught up with My Li and found themselves no closer to regaining the seal of the Triad, the friction between their disparate personalities and their different approaches to solving their problems, which had been building up since they received their instructions from the White Fan, erupted into open conflict.

My Li lay listening to their struggle as the Red Poles fought and cursed, letting out their months of bottled up aggression, animosity and ill-will towards one another.

'You fool! I won't let you kill him!' Yung said in a voice that My Li could tell was constricted. Unknown to My Li, Chang's vice-like hands were around Yung's throat.

'He is our only hope.'

'You white-livered, chicken hearted apology for a Red Pole. What does it matter of he dies or we die. We are all going to die someday! What matters is not when but how you die!'

There could only be one outcome to this contest. Yung was engaged in an unequal encounter and was no match against Chang's bludgeoning blows.

'Help me!'

My Li heard Yung appeal to Lau and the other of the dwarf's men who had returned from taking Kinqua and Simone to the cave. But, as the Red Poles strove for the upper hand, there was no sound of extra feet rushing to join in the fray. My Li heard a heavy thud followed by a groan. For a full minute My Li did not know which of the Red Poles had toppled the other. He heard only heavy breathing. Then his heart sank as Chang spoke and he knew that Yung, the lesser of two evils so far as My Li was concerned, had been vanquished by his more dangerous partner.

'Take them both up to the cave.'

'Both?' queried Lau, incredulous.

'You heard me. Take both of them and tie up Yung as you've already done with the others. I am through with him. Let this be a lesson to you if you want to succeed in the Triad. Don't even trust your comrades!'

My Li lay still while the dwarf's men moved to obey Chang.

'He's tied,' Lau told Chang when they finished.

Yung moaned and My Li almost felt the thud as Chang sank his foot in Yung's ribs.

'Get up! Get up I say!'

Yung must have been dazed as he suddenly said, 'What is this? Why am I tied up? What are you doing?' as he realised he was bound for the first time.

'I'll tell you what I'm doing,' said Chang, his resolve and determination obvious in his voice. 'I'm going on alone! I'm not going to be held back by some namby-pamby new recruit who goes to water when it really matters! Now get them both out of my sight while I work out what to do next!'

My Li was dragged to his feet and, trussed like birds, he and Yung floundered clumsily up the slope towards the fold in the rock face where Kinqua and Simone had been taken. Loose stones skidded out from under their feet and went careering back down behind them, almost causing My Li to lose balance and topple over. On the first occasion he slipped, one of the dwarf's men caught and steadied him. But on the second, he lost his footing on the rough rocks and fell. Fortunately, Lau was behind him and caught his arm, saving him from falling bound to the bottom.

'The blindfold,' appealed My Li. 'I can't see where I'm going.'

'Take it off him,' ordered Lau, and the man with the goatee obliged.

My Li opened and closed his eyes to get them used to the glare.

The man with the goatee stared at My Li's injured features. 'Another session with Chang and you won't have any face left to bruise. Why don't you tell him where you've hidden the ring and then we can all go home?'

'Because I honestly don't know,' slurred My Li.

Lau pushed My Li in the small of the back. 'Come on. Get a move on. We haven't got all day.'

At the top of the rubble they could look back the way they had come. Chang was standing deep in thought at the bottom. In front of them was an overhanging ledge of rock. The cliff face under the overhang was covered in Aboriginal rock paintings depicting kangaroos, spearmen, an enormous coiled snake and motifs of religious significance. There were dozens of hand stencils, created by the painter holding his hand against the rock and, after spreading the fingers, spraying a solution of ochre and water from his mouth over his hand. When the hand was removed, its outline remained on the surface of the rock. My Li had seen similar artwork while walking through Heaven's Gate. My Li used the sight of the paintings as an excuse to pause and catch his breath while at the same time take stock of his surroundings, but the dwarf's men would not have it and propelled him forward, to a small ledge at the top of the scree slope. The ledge was dominated by an oval shaped boulder about a metre and a half in height, and My Li observed that the boulder obscured the entrance to a cave.

My Li and Yung waited with Lau's rifle aimed at them while the other dwarf's men put their shoulders and weight to the boulder. My Li was in no condition or mental state to resist and the Red Pole was bewildered by his sudden change in circumstances.

Because of the elongated shape of the boulder, it only rolled a third of its circumference before coming to rest but the movement was far enough to expose the dark opening of the cave. My Li noted that the ledge in front of the cave had a raised lip which prevented the boulder from toppling over and rolling down the scree slope. Once inside the cave the boulder would be rolled back across the exit. Below the ledge, all the way to the base of the rock, was the clutter of rubble that had fallen from further up the rock face. Both My Li and Yung were thrust into the cave.

They had to bend over to enter.

Simone's eyes registered shock as she saw My Li's condition and fear and amazement as she saw Yung following him but bound like themselves. My Li tripped and slumped to his knees. The interior of the cave was about four or five metres square and the floor was smooth with wear.

Outside, the dwarf's men rolled the boulder back across the entrance – like a cork stopping the neck of a bottle. They were as securely imprisoned as if they had been put into a cell. The rock blocked most of the daylight from entering and the lack of light turned the cave into a dingy tomb.

A little light did manage to enter the cave where the shape of the boulder did not correspond to the cave opening. But the thin rays of brightness that pierced the gloomy interior were faint and few, like My Li's fading hopes for their survival.

CHAPTER TWENTY-EIGHT

My Li, Kinqua, Simone and Yung, the disgraced Red Pole, sat bound on the floor of the cave. As his eyes attuned to the dimness, My Li could make out Kinqua's anxious but smiling face; Simone's pert features registered relief to see him but distress at his condition. Yung's mouth was slack and his face blank with amazement.

'Chang will leave us here to rot!' mourned Yung. 'And be commended and promoted for our murders...'

'The net of Heaven eventually catches all wrongdoers,' Kinqua said to console him.

'Don't expect any sympathy from me,' snapped Simone. 'What is he doing here with us anyway?'

My Li explained.

He had to speak slowly to make himself understood, so badly battered was his mouth. 'After what I just went through, if that is the worst his friend Chang does to me, I will die happy.'

'Let's not talk of dying,' said Kinqua. 'Let us apply our brains to how we can get out of here. If you are feeling up to it My Li, with three men here we should be able to brace our feet against the boulder blocking the entrance and push it away.'

'You won't be able to,' Yung told them. 'The ledge outside has a raised lip that locks the rock into place once it is rolled in front of the entrance. We discovered the cave when we arrived here this morning.

The rock fits so neatly it looks like the savages have used the cave as a prison or storehouse for centuries.'

'Did you plan to imprison us here this morning,' asked Simone.

'Yes,' admitted Yung.

'And now you find yourself in it!'

'Yes.'

'Fate works in wonderful ways,' reflected Kinqua.

'It serves you right,' said Simone.

Yung nodded in agreement in the gloom. 'I regret what has happened. I now rue the day I became a member of the brotherhood. I did not know all it entailed.'

'I don't believe you,' scoffed Simone. 'You seemed as pleased to see us as your friend...'

'I knew what becoming a member of the Triad might involve but thought I could avoid its less pleasant aspects while still reaping the rewards and benefits of being one of the brotherhood. But it is impossible. Now I realise that evil spreads like a stain and that once a fabric is touched by it, it tints all of the cloth, not just parts of it. The last thing I ever wanted to do was to come to this heathen land!'

'Why did you then?'

'Because we had to. There is death sentence on both of us if we fail to return the ring. If it wasn't for fear of my life, I would have walked away from the brotherhood long ago.'

'A death sentence! No wonder you did not give up trying to find us,' said Kinqua in astonishment.

'Surely no-one would know if you simply took another identity and disappeared?' asked My Li.

'The Triad has ears and eyes in every corner of the world.'

'I think you've got what you deserve,' said Simone.

'Leave him be,' said Kinqua. 'His suffering will be as great as ours.'

'The girl is right,' said Yung. 'I deserve to share your fate.'

My Li raised himself on his elbow:

'He tried to help me Simone! That's why he's in here with us!'

'It might be a trick,' said Simone. 'It might be a ploy to find out if we really have the ring or not.'

'Believe me,' said My Li. 'If I had the ring, I would have willingly handed it over to them an hour ago.'

'I knew what becoming a brother might entail,' Yung said remorsefully. 'I knew it all along in my heart but the head sometimes does not hear what the heart is trying to tell it. My falling out with Chang has been coming for some time. I have always found Chang unnecessarily over-zealous in his work.'

Yung sounded so downcast and disconsolate My Li was moved to comfort him. 'If you listen to your heart, you will learn nothing but good things, for the heart is a fountain that tosses up droplets of wisdom to the brain.'

Kinqua smiled in the blackness. He had used the same words to comfort My Li in the hold on board the Dayspring.

'Let us try to move the rock,' suggested Kinqua.

'It won't work.' Yung told him dejectedly.

'Let us at least try!' insisted Kinqua.

By lying on their backs, and with Simone joining in to help, they placed their feet against the boulder and pushed with all their might. It did not budge. There was not even an encouraging quiver or scrape of rock against rock.

'It is no use.'

'Try again.'

They tried again. The rock still resisted their efforts.

'It isn't going to move. This cave is going to become our burial place.'

'It already is for those poor souls at the back of the cave.'

My Li stared at the rear wall of the cave. He had not previously noticed the white bones and human skulls in the niches and recesses hewn from the rock. The cave was an Aboriginal catacomb.

'Greater men and women than we have been interred in less salubrious sepulchres,' said Kinqua.

'That may be so,' said Simone, 'but if I have to spend the last hours of my life listening to you three feeling sorry for yourselves and philosophising, I will die of nausea not starvation. Let's concentrate on getting ourselves out of here! I haven't survived all that I have to die in a cave. I am not ready to curl up my toes as yet!'

The light shafting through the gap around the boulder blocking the entrance began to fade as the late afternoon light gave way to dusk.

Soon it was pitch black inside the cave and, unable to move the rock, their mood became increasingly pessimistic.

'What a way to die,' lamented Yung. 'No-one to mourn our passing. No-one to light candles for us or perform rites in our names...'

'At least we won't suffocate...' said Simone.

'Chang might decide to slit out throats..'

'Unless... ' mused Kinqua.

'Unless what?' prompted My Li.

'That slope of rubble...?'

'What about it?'

'I was wondering how stable is the ledge the boulder across the entrance is resting on?'

'Why? What are you getting at?'

'If the ledge was to give way, then the boulder would tumble down the slope and we would be free.'

'But our hands would still be tied.'

'Our feet could function. If we could get away from here and gain ourselves some time, we could find a way of getting loose.'

'But the ledge is solid. What can we do to encourage it to collapse?'

'The ledge seems solid. But it is resting on unstable stones…'

'So?'

'If the stones that are supporting the ledge were removed, the ledge would be undermined and the weight of the boulder might be more than the ledge can hold on its own. It might, with luck, break away.'

'Marvellous,' said My Li. I'll go outside and dig away the stones. You wait here while I do it!' he said sarcastically. 'How in heaven's name do you expect the rocks to be conveniently removed from under the ledge, Kinqua? Sometimes you astound me!'

'With vibrations,' came Kinqua's voice through the dark.

'Vibrations?'

'It only requires one stone to move to start an avalanche. One stone collides with another, which collides with another – until the whole mass begins to slide.'

'How do we convince the first stone to obligingly collide with its neighbour?' gibed My Li, the pain from his finger and bruises making him irritable and disparaging towards what he saw as Kinqua's esoteric and unrealistic suggestion.

'As I said before – with vibrations.'

'Explain what you are thinking to us, Kinqua?' encouraged Simone.

'I have seen the saffron-coloured robed Buddhist monks compel their tubular bells to ring solely by the sound of their prayers. Once in a temple, I watched while some monks continuously chanted a single note until the air itself vibrated and the bells rang of their own accord…'

225

'Is that what you would like us to do?'

'It might work. It might cause the rocks to move.'

'I have heard of European opera singers singing notes so shrill that they cause glasses to crack and break. Is that similar to what you are thinking of Kinqua?' asked Simone.

Yes.'

'It is said, in the mountain ranges of Tibet, that landslides and snow-slips can be started by the noise of the flight of a solitary bird as it soars among the passes. When I watched the monks, they chanted the sound 'om', holding the note as long as they could and gradually building the resonance and volume until objects and statuettes on the shelves quivered ... and then the bells began to ring. If we do the same, perhaps we will be able to cause the rubble to move...'

'Let us try it. What other hope do we have? If nothing else, it will give us something to do. At least until Chang decides what he intends to do with us,' urged Simone.

'No. I think it is a ridiculous idea. Count me out,' said My Li.

'Ridiculous?' repeated Kinqua. 'Sometimes what seems silly and ludicrous today becomes tomorrow's reality and commonplace. If people were not prepared to be seen as ridiculous, most of the world's inventions would never have seen the light of day...'

'I'm sorry Kinqua. I think we would be wasting what little time remains of us,' My Li said wearily. 'It won't work.'

'If you believe it will work My Li, it might.'

'No Kinqua. I don't believe in miracles. I have helped alleviate the pain of many ill and dying people with my apothecary's craft but what is ordained always comes to pass.'

'But who is to say what was ordained unless you seek alternatives? You can choose to be optimistic or negative in life My Li. But if you choose negativity, then, like a lodestone or magnet, you will attract that which is negative.'

My Li did not answer.

For almost an hour they sat silent in the dark. Then Simone said, 'Kinqua; if you would like to attempt your chant, I will sing with you if you wish.'

A moment or two later Yung added his support: 'I will sing with you too Kinqua – if you will allow me to?'

Kinqua, Simone and Yung waited to hear if My Li was going to add his agreement to their own, but My Li was struggling with his demons in the dark. Overcome by despair, My Li was melancholically reliving the series of events that had brought him, and his friends, to their current harrowing predicament. His mother's financial difficulties and her terminal illness; Tiao's terrible death; the appalling conditions on the Dayspring; forced labour on MacArthur's sheep-run; the massacre of Baracoona's tribesmen; Lun-Tan's murder, and now this.

Preoccupied with his own disheartened state of mind, My Li was oblivious to all but his own despondency. When Kinqua, Simone and Yung began to hum the 'om' sound, My Li was taken by surprise. Roused from his lethargy, he listened as his two friends, and the Red Pole sharing their incarceration, held the hum, their lips trembling, for as long as their breath allowed, and then repeated the sound. After a few minutes their voices synchronised and found a comfortable pitch that reverberated around the rock walls of the cave. As Kinqua, Simone and Yung's voices grew in volume and mutual confidence, the cave rang to the sound of their harmonic humming, and as My Li listened, he felt as if they were willing him to help them.

Casting aside his depressed state, My Li, tentatively at first, and then with increasing commitment and resonance, reached out to his friends and joined in their chanting until their four voices were in unison. And as the sound soared and echoed and rang around what was a perfect echo chamber, emphasising the tone and timbre of their voices, My Li was gripped by a fierce surge of elation and positivity.

227

My Li's involvement spurred the others to even greater intensity. The air inside the cave became charged, like the atmosphere before an approaching electrical storm. Simone later swore she felt the ether quiver in response to their incessant throbbing hum.

Simone shuddered involuntarily as something tickled her on the nape of her neck and then trickled down her back. Without slackening her participation in their chorus, Simone realised their vocal efforts had dislodged granules of sand or dirt from the roof of the cave above their heads.

Then she heard a clatter beyond the boulder, and the receding tinkle of a rock as it fell, bounding down the slope of unstable stones. My Li, Simone, Kinqua and Yung kept up their sonorous humming, and another rock, followed by another, clicked and pattered down the incline. The individual sounds of falling rocks grew in number and then blended into a swelling rumble. The floor to the cave trembled under its occupants. Suddenly, Simone was aware that the cave was alive with dust and flying particles, and where the darkness that was the boulder had previously prevented her from staring into the night sky, she found herself gazing, dumbfounded, at a dazzling array of stars.

CHAPTER TWENTY-NINE

Baracoona had not been slowed by the need to carry provisions for his unremitting chase like My Li and the Red Poles. Where the others saw only emptiness and a terrain unable to sustain life, Baracoona lived in luxury off the land.

Baracoona's people had, eons ago, adapted to their harsh environment. Where Europeans and Orientals saw only unappetising and unattractive stunted and prickly plants striving to survive under adverse conditions, Baracoona's people saw food. They knew of over one hundred and forty different plants available to be eaten in what to others was desert. Besides eating marsupials, rock pythons, goannas and bustard birds, they ground grass seeds in wooden bowls and ate the fruit of trees – such as the quandong – and the roots of others in the form of edible tubers and yams.

They nurtured the native game by burning off the sparse vegetation with fire-sticks, thus encouraging new growth; and they celebrated being alive with ceremonial gatherings or corroborees. Even ants represented a major food source for Baracoona. The previous evening he had feasted on honey ants. In a region where sweet foods were few and far between, the honey ants were considered a delicacy. The honey ants collect nectar from the leaves of acacia bushes and transfer the juice to storage ants that remain deep in their underground nests.

Storage ants grow to be as big as small grapes – black ants with their abdomens swollen up to four times the size of their head and thorax combined.

Baracoona had dug into a nest and plucked out the storage ants, nipping off their sweet abdomens with his teeth. Other kinds of ants also provided sustenance or services. Green ants had nippers that could be used as sutures to close cuts. But the bull ants – meat eating scavengers that could reduce a dead creature to its skeleton, and which were capable of inflicting bites, stings and welts which, en masse could kill, Baracoona avoided with respect.

Two days earlier Baracoona had come across the carcass of the pony and the cooking fire where it had been butchered and eaten. An eagle had been tearing at the animal's entrails and armies of ants were already carrying away infinitesimal pieces of flesh to their nests to feed their queen. The pony's hide was turning to leather in the sun.

Baracoona had almost caught up with the creators of the footsteps he had been following for so long. Earlier in his pursuit, the wind had had time to erode and degrade the edges around any imprint in the soil or sand but now the footprints were clearly delineated. He did not like to travel at night, especially across country inhabited by foreign tribes, where spirits he did not know how to placate might be abroad. Nonetheless, his rapid progress by day whittled down the three to five days start the Red Poles and My Li, Kinqua and their companions respectively had on him. As Baracoona steadily reduced the interval between them, his solitary progress was accompanied by mixed emotions.

The warrior was concerned. Concerned because it was obvious to him that the Red Poles and the three men with them were in hot pursuit of My Li and his friends, and Baracoona had no way of knowing whether My Li and his companions knew they were in danger.

Baracoona suspected they did not, and he worried that the yellow man with the mutilated nose might overtake My Li and Kinqua before he could catch up to them or warn his friends of the danger.

He was also looking forward to renewing his acquaintance with My Li and Kinqua and his pleasure was compounded by the knowledge that every pace took him closer to the land of his birth, for My Li's course was taking him into the heart of Baracoona's homeland. Somewhere in the wide expanse of sand and spinifex Baracoona's relations and friends were either camped by a water source or journeying to another one in order to avoid completely depleting nearby food supplies – or of wiping out game in its vicinity. Baracoona correctly surmised that My Li needed his assistance and was looking for him. But by doing so, My Li had drawn the murderous Red Poles into territory where their presence threatened his own kind.

The feeling that most dominated Baracoona's sensibilities was that of grim expectation. Since leaving Heaven's Gate, his activities had been motivated by his need to avenge his tribesmen's tragic deaths. Revenge had been the sole reason he remained near Lambing Flat. Baracoona had hovered like a vengeful angel, waiting for the chance to settle his account with the Red Poles. Now the time had come, and Baracoona crooned songs that would add strength to his throwing arm, make his aim keen and fill him with fortitude when he ultimately came face to face with the killers. He languidly loped along, looking forward to the confrontation he knew must eventuate within hours.

As the sun sank, Baracoona had no doubt My Li had walked into a trap. He had read the signs at the boulders he knew as the landmark called 'the place where the Rainbow Serpent laid its eggs'. He had pored over the scuff marks and dislodged stones until he knew almost exactly what had occurred. Baracoona saw that the Red Poles had overtaken My Li, Kinqua and whoever else was with them. And he realised that My Li was now following the Red Poles. Baracoona had stood thoughtfully before the cairn that had been raised over Mark the midshipman's body. He knew from the sickly stench that rose from the rocks that there was a decaying corpse under the stones.

From an examination of the tracks leading away from the place of the Rainbow Serpent's Eggs, Baracoona was able to learn who was missing. All of the Red Poles' party had gone on. My Li, Kinqua and a third set of prints were distinguishable as having also continued. The fourth person with My Li's group was beneath the cairn. The stick cross Kinqua had placed in the rocks piled over Mark's head was still *in situ* and Baracoona was aware the cross was associated with death by the Europeans.

Baracoona did not want to disturb and desecrate the grave and, consequently, had no idea whether the occupant had been killed by the Red Poles or died of natural causes. He had certainly not died of thirst, as the water-hole in the rock was surrounded by marks left by My Li's friends as they crouched to drink. Baracoona has been pleased to see the vegetation had been replaced over the cistern in the rock. He was also thrilled to note that someone else had been in the proximity of the place of the Rainbow Serpent's Eggs. Judging from the few indications of the other person's presence, the fact that whoever it might be was barefooted, and the length of stride that revealed the person responsible for the tracks was moving rapidly and purposefully, Baracoona surmised the stranger was most likely one of his own kinsmen.

As Baracoona set off across the desert, his eyes glued to the ground, he knew precisely where both parties of the intruders into his tribal territory were heading – to the red rock holding the sky above the earth.

Only a third of the orb of the sun remained above the horizon by the time Baracoona saw the sacred place in the distance. Every crevice, crack and marking on the rock held religious significance to Baracoona and, bathed in the reddish glow of the sinking sun, the rock beckoned him like a beacon. The intermingled tracks of My Li's and the Red Poles' parties led straight towards the immense hump rising above the desert. The thorny lizards, whose fierce appearance disguised their timid nature, scurried to get out of the determined Aboriginal's way.

Being so close to what he knew must be his destination, Baracoona braved the encroaching dark. He was back on familiar territory and the spirits that walked abroad after the sunset were mostly those friendly to him. But to make sure he was protected from any supernatural maliciousness, he recited an incantation to ward off potential harm. Above him, the stars popped into the darkening evening sky, one after the other, until the Milky Way, crystal clear in the desert night air, was so thick with sparkling pin-pricks of light, it threatened to become too heavy to stay aloft and to fall to earth. Baracoona noted the Pleiades constellation, which his tribe believed represented young women searching for food, was starkly luminous to his naked eye. They were being courted by the young men of Orion, out hunting among the stars.

Baracoona saw none of his own tribe as he sped towards the rock. But as he neared the base, he saw the flicker of a fire and turned towards it. Dark shapes rose up around him.

CHAPTER THIRTY

After ordering Yung and My Li to be shut up with the comfort girl and the old man, Chang instructed the dwarf's men to take turns guarding the mouth of the cave. But neither Lau nor the others were keen to spend the after dark hours taking turns to be alone in the eerie precincts of the prisoners' cave. The dwarf's men were ill-educated and supernaturally credulous. The last thing they wanted was to expose themselves to the shamanistic wizardry they believed the Aboriginals were capable of – especially as the red rock was, judging from the plentiful paintings, obviously hallowed ground.

Instead, they praised the cave as being a natural gaol, claiming that it was pointless to keep watch, as once the boulder was in place across the opening, it was immoveable. Chang, already a troubled man and now anxious not to encourage further mutiny, relented and allowed the men to keep each other company by the fire they lit to ward off the chilly desert night air, and to keep unwelcome Aboriginal spirits at bay.

Chang was still pondering how to solve his predicament. The new Red Pole recruit, Yung, had been found wanting when the chips were down. He had lacked obduracy and the necessary hardness of heart to be a true soldier of the Triad.

Yung was expendable, as was anyone else who got in the way of the Triad. And if Chang could retrieve the seal, he would return alone to be lauded by his colleagues and receive kudos from his superiors. He still had time to find the savage and the seal. Once the ring was found, he could send word through the dwarf that he was returning, albeit late, with his prize.

The idea of returning to China and the acclaim of the lodge appealed to Chang. The question was, unfortunately for Chang, where was the ring?

Lau recommended torturing My Li until he revealed the location. 'He knows where the seal is. Pull out his toe-nails. He will talk then. You wait and see! You won't be able to stop him.'

The young man with the goatee beard was taking his turn to boil the rice for their meal over the fire. 'Bring the girl down. She must know what happened to the ring. I could make her talk.'

'What about the grey-beard? He might value his remaining years more than the widow's son?' advised the third of the dwarf's men.

'A waste of time!' declared Lau. 'He is old and frail. He will join his ancestors as soon as you hit him. Concentrate on the widow's son.'

Chang pretended to ignore their council but he weighed their words and came to his own conclusion.

'I have decided. We will eat and then bring him down – and the girl. If he is telling the truth about giving the ring away, then I must learn the name of the Aboriginal to whom it was given and where I will find him. The widow's son has shown he is strong willed but I doubt he will enjoy seeing his young female friend suffer because he refuses to tell us his secret.'

'What shall we do with them when we have learnt what we need to know?' asked the young man with the goatee.

'I don't care. Put them back in the cave and let their bones mingle with those of the savages.'

The goatee bearded man grinned. 'I can think of better things to do with the girl.'

'Do what you will,' said Chang. 'Once I have the information I need, I will have no further use for any of them. The widow's son will be mine to kill. Do with the others as you wish.'

The man with the goatee beard's grin widened in anticipation as he received Chang's permission to do as he pleased with their female prisoner.

Chang's chopsticks were poised in front of his open mouth when they first heard the sighing moan coming from the direction of the cave. The noise had a spectral, liturgical quality that, being in the shrine-like surroundings of the rock, sounded strange and uncanny, and made their blood freeze with fear.

Startled, the dwarf's men put their rice bowls aside and reached for their firearms. Chang rose to his feet, facing the source of the sound.

'It's coming from somewhere near the cave! Get up there and make sure everything is alright.'

Lau and the man with the goatee beard looked at Chang as if he was mad. The whites of their eyes were enlarged and fearful in the firelight.

'Not me,' said Lau. 'They're your prisoners! You go and check them out.'

'Who knows what that might be!' quavered the man with the goatee beard, looking over his shoulder into the dark.

'I'll go,' said the third of the dwarf's men, and he stood and pushed his pistol more firmly into his belt.

He would be the first to die.

At the edge of the extent of their firelight, where the glow from the flames was overwhelmed by the blackness surrounding their oasis of light, stood the figure of an aboriginal. The Aborigine was armed with four spears tipped with quartz chipped until razor sharp. One of the spears was already nestled in his woomera or throwing stick. It was aggressively aligned on the Chinese around the fire. The hum from the cave helped make his appearance ghoulish and disconcerting.

'I am Baracoona,' he said in his own tongue. 'I am the keeper of this sacred place. He whom you killed is now a ghost returned from the dead to avenge his kinsmen. I have come to claim my vengeance.'

There, glinting against Baracoona's chest whenever it caught the firelight, was the seal of the Black Scarf Triad. The ring Chang had been seeking for so long. Chang could not wrench his eyes away from it.

Baracoona's right arm arched and threw the first of his spears with a movement so fast the action was a blur to those who saw it. The dwarf's man about to investigate the noise from the direction of the cave gasped in surprise at the three metre shaft protruding from his heart. Another bloody metre of point and shaft stuck out of his back. He sank slowly to his knees. By the time he died, Baracoona's second spear had already impaled the man with the goatee. The spear had transfixed him through the neck and he clawed at the light stem of the grass tree plant that made such excellent lightweight and straight shafts for the Aboriginals' spears, croaking like a frog being devoured by a snake.

Lau received a respite of seconds before Baracoona turned his attention to him. Lau grabbed his loaded rifle. Its barrel was lifting up and towards Baracoona when the hum from the cave was blotted out by the noise of the loose stones and gravel collapsing.

He heard the ledge break with a large crack, and, as the boulder blocking the entrance to the cave bounded and bounced down the scree slope behind Chang's camp and thudded out into the scrub, Lau was distracted for a fatal fraction of a second. It was all the delay Baracoona required. His third spear penetrated Lau's stomach, and its impact caused Lau to squeeze the trigger, firing the weapon harmlessly into the night air. With Lau groaning and clutching at the spear in his abdomen beside him, Chang, whose attention had also been momentarily diverted by the boulder bursting into the undergrowth, snatched his dagger from his belt and hurled himself at Baracoona. But out of the darkness appeared other armed Aboriginal's. There were at least a dozen warriors.

One moment Baracoona was alone, and the next, materialising noiselessly out of the night, his tribesmen were standing either side of him. Chang could not approach their spears and live. The proud Red Pole waited helplessly as the Aboriginals formed a ring around him and slowly tightened their human noose.

The bearded Aboriginal who had shown My Li, Kinqua and Simone the way to the rock was the first to reach the vicinity of the cave. My Li, Simone and Yung had already scrambled clear of the entrance. The scree slope had slumped as Kinqua had hoped and the unsupported ledge had snapped under the weight of the boulder. The air was still thick with dust.

On seeing Yung, the bearded Aborigine flung back his throwing arm, a barbed spear already clenched by its butt in his woomera.

'No! Spare him!' cried My Li and he placed himself in front of Yung. The bearded warrior grunted unhappily but lowered his spear. He continued to hold it pointed at Yung's throat with one hand while he sliced through the twine that bound the prisoners' hands behind their backs with a blade of chipped stone in the other.

My Li and Simone massaged and flexed their cramped arms and hands to encourage their circulation.

'Kinqua?'

Simone had realised Kinqua was not with them and that he had not yet emerged from the cave. My Li frantically scrabbled up the debris of the scree slope, even more difficult to negotiate since the avalanche. My Li's feet fought for purchase and he was forced to clamber on all fours to get to the opening.

Kinqua had not moved.

His hands were still bound and he was sitting in his favoured lotus position. Another Aboriginal came up the loose stones with more agility and less difficulty than My Li. He was holding a fire-stick. As the light danced around the inside of the cave, Kinqua did not move. My Li knelt before his elderly friend and felt for the carotid artery in Kinqua's neck. There was no pulse. My Li bowed his head until it reached the cool rock of the floor of the cave.

It was another week before My Li, Simone and Yung left the locality of the rock. My Li had refused to mourn Kinqua's death in the normal Chinese fashion. Instead, he had sponged the dirt from his body and, after washing and drying Kinqua's cotton clothes, dressed him again before interring him, with the help of Baracoona's kinsmen, in the cave in which he had met his end.

After lying Kinqua on one of the rock shelves in the cave, My Li sat with him for a long time before rejoining Simone and Baracoona. Simone was crying when My Li came back from the cave.

'Please don't cry for him,' My Li gently admonished her. 'Kinqua would not have wanted us to be sad and sorrowful for him.'

'I'm not,' said Simone. 'I'm crying for what we have lost. I'm crying for myself.'

Simone looked up tearfully at My Li. His eyes were wet but he was smiling broadly at her.

'See!' said Simone. 'You're trying to be brave and manly but you are on the verge of crying yourself!'

'Ah!' said My Li. 'These are not tears of mourning you see in my eyes. These are tears of joy. For we have been privileged to know a great person. Greatness is not only measured by wealth, power and prestige …'

In front of the entrance to the cave fluttered two pennants on poles. Instead of the usual prayer flags, My Li had tied the scarves that had been found on Yung and Chang. The black scarves with the motif of the Triad in white on one corner.

All three of the dwarf's men had died from wounds Baracoona had inflicted on them. Lau lingered in agony till dawn. When My Li looked upon their corpses the nest morning, Chang's body was not among them.

'What happened to the man with the scarred nose?' My Li asked Baracoona.

Baracoona pointed to the enormous ant hills standing nearby. One of the three metre high nests had been neatly lopped off below its apex and the top then replaced. Sticking out where the cut off top had carefully been put back, was the ankle and foot of a man. The foot was shod and the shoe badly worn to its outside. Baracoona's men had hollowed out part of the ant hill and buried Chang alive, upside down inside it.

Baracoona walked with My Li, Simone and Yung and the bearded Aborigine who was to be their guide until they had left Baracoona's tribal country – as far as the low ridge overlooking the rock. Baracoona remained leaning on his spear while Simone, My Li, Yung and their guide set out for the horizon.

When My Li and Simone turned to wave, Baracoona responded by holding his arm uplifted in the air, and then he was gone.

My Li had given Baracoona back his tjurunga and asked for the ring in return.

When the time came for My Li and Simone to separate from Yung, My Li handed the seal that had caused him so much misery to the Red Pole who was pledged to take it back to China. Yung gratefully accepted the ring.

'I will ensure it reaches the land of our ancestors. Then, so far as the Triad is concerned, you will be deceased, and of no further interest for them.'

'And you?'

'Somehow I will ensure that my first task will also be my last. What will you both do?'

'Walk on!' said My Li. 'We will walk on!'

The Red Pole named Yung watched My Li and Simone until they were swallowed by the shimmering heat haze. Then, patting the ring in his pocket to remind himself that his task was accomplished, he too went on his way to the coast, and a ship.

In distant China, as yet unaware of the recovery of the ring, the lodge of the Black Scarf Triad had gathered for another ceremony. Eighteen months to the day had passed since the Red Poles set out on their quest and, although reports had reached the White Fan of their arrival in the Great South Land, and of the presence of the youth who had stolen the ring, no word had been received confirming the safety of the seal. The eighteen months had flown by too speedily for the lodge's ex-Master of Ceremonies, the merchant Han Ying.

Stripped of all insignia of his previous rank, the disgraced and distraught ex-Master of Ceremonies, his nails bitten to their quick, was brought into the courtyard, the same courtyard where the new recruit had been accepted by his brethren. Eighteen months to the day, the Triad had been instructed to assemble to witness Han Ying's Death from One Thousand Cuts.

Made in the USA
Charleston, SC
25 October 2013